Left Out

"You don't seem very happy," Ellen said. "I guess it isn't much fun having to hobble around all the time."

"I'm not hobbling!" Jessica protested, putting down her sandwich. She'd lost her appetite. "I guess I'm getting a little tired of it," she admitted. "There are so many things I feel like doing, and it's no fun being left out."

"I know," Ellen said feelingly.

But Jessica wasn't sure she did *know. Ellen had never been left out of anything! Until that week, Jessica hadn't been either.*

She didn't like it. Not one little bit.

SWEET VALLEY TWINS

One of the Gang

Written by
Jamie Suzanne

Created by
FRANCINE PASCAL

A BANTAM SKYLARK BOOK®
TORONTO • NEW YORK • LONDON • SYDNEY • AUCKLAND

RL 4, 008–012

ONE OF THE GANG
A Bantam Skylark Book / August 1987

Sweet Valley High is a registered trademark of Francine Pascal.
Sweet Valley Twins is a trademark of Francine Pascal.

Conceived by Francine Pascal
Produced by Cloverdale Press Inc.,
133 Fifth Ave., New York, N.Y. 10003

Cover art by James Mathewuse

Skylark Books is a registered trademark of Bantam Books, Inc.
Registered in U.S. Patent and Trademark Office and elsewhere.

ISBN 0-553-15531-8

Published simultaneously in the United States and Canada

Bantam Books are published by Bantam Books, Inc. Its trademark, consisting of the words "Bantam Books" and the portrayal of a rooster, is Registered in U.S. Patent and Trademark Office and in other countries. Marca Registrada. Bantam Books, Inc., 666 Fifth Avenue, New York, New York 10103.

PRINTED IN THE UNITED STATES OF AMERICA

O 0 9 8 7 6 5 4 3 2 1

One of the Gang

One

"Liz, can you come over here for a sec?" Jessica Wakefield asked her twin sister. "I'm stuck on this stupid math problem!"

It was Monday afternoon, and Jessica was doing her homework at the table in the Wakefields' Spanish-styled kitchen. California sunlight streamed through the windows. The twins' older brother, Steven, was working on his homework too—and driving Jessica and Elizabeth crazy at the same time! Steven was fourteen—two years older than the twins—and could be close to impossible at times. Just that day, out of the blue, he'd informed them that he had ESP—extrasensory perception—and had already "foreseen" everything they said or did.

"I knew you'd have problems with your

homework, Jess," Steven said now, looking smug. "My ESP is at work again."

Elizabeth, who was spooning the last bit of chocolate-chip batter onto a cookie sheet, couldn't help grinning. "I'm not sure you'd need ESP to guess Jessica was going to have trouble with math," she pointed out.

"What are you talking about?" Jessica said to her brother. "You're really getting weird, Steven. Do you know that?"

"I'm not weird," Steven objected. "I'm special, that's all. I happen to have ESP. In fact, I had my very first vision of the future this morning."

Jessica glared at him. "The only thing extra about you is that you're extra obnoxious," she said.

Elizabeth laughed. "Can you really see into the future?"

Jessica groaned. "Of course he can't," she wailed. "Liz, don't encourage him!"

Elizabeth slid the cookie sheet into the oven. "I'll help you in a minute," she told her twin. "Let me clean up over here first."

Jessica's blue-green eyes flashed with impatience. Sometimes she couldn't understand her twin's behavior at all. Imagine actually cleaning up after baking cookies! Jessica always left the dirty dishes in a pile for someone else to take care of. But, as the twins' mother often remarked, Jessica and Elizabeth weren't one bit identical when it came to personalities.

As far as looks went, it was virtually impossible to tell them apart, from their long blond hair and blue-green eyes to the dimple each girl showed when she smiled. But Elizabeth, who was four minutes older, often thought of herself as the "big sister." Conscientious in everything she did, she really *liked* working hard at school. Elizabeth was very active on *The Sweet Valley Sixers,* the sixth-grade newspaper. Jessica, on the other hand, wouldn't have wasted a second on something as boring as the school paper. She was much too busy with the Boosters, a cheerleading squad to which she belonged, and the Unicorns, a special group of girls whom Elizabeth and her best friend Amy Sutton considered snobs. Jessica loved the Unicorns. Lately she had been trying to think of new ways to impress Janet Howell, the eighth-grade president of the club.

"You don't believe I have ESP," Steven said, looking as if his feelings were hurt. "I don't think that's fair, Jessica. I didn't tell you, but I happen to have predicted that you'd be appointed chairman of the Mini Olympics committee."

Jessica tossed back her hair. "Well, *anyone* could have guessed I was going to be chosen. I'm perfect for the job, aren't I?"

"It must have been your modesty that made Mr. Butler decide to put you in charge," Steven said with a playful smile.

Elizabeth came over to join them at the table. "I think you'll do a great job, Jess," she said.

"You'll probably put together the best Mini Olympics the lower school has ever seen!"

The Mini Olympics were an annual tradition in Sweet Valley. Each year the sixth graders organized the day-long festival for the younger grades. The fifth and sixth graders also joined in the competitions, which included every kind of sport and relay event imaginable. Mr. Butler, the physical education teacher at the lower school, was the faculty advisor for this year's Mini Olympics. As student chairman, Jessica would be working closely with Mr. Butler to decide which events should be kept in from the previous years and which new events should be added. Jessica knew she could do a great job, and she had a feeling Janet Howell would be really impressed. Jessica wanted more than anything to be praised by the members of the Unicorn Club—and she was sure this would do it!

"My ESP tells me I'm going to be late for basketball practice if I don't get out of here," Steven said suddenly, slamming his history book shut and jumping up from the table. "See you two later!" He gave Jessica a serious look. "I'm getting that weird feeling again, Jess. I think you should make sure to stay inside today. Otherwise . . ." He let his voice trail off ominously.

"He's giving me the creeps," Jessica said when Steven had bounded out of the room. "How can we get him to stop this ESP nonsense? I can't stand it!"

Elizabeth looked thoughtful. "I know what

you mean. I think we may have to think of some way to get him to stop. He's getting to be a real pain."

"Who's getting to be a pain?" Mrs. Wakefield asked, opening the screen door and coming into the kitchen with her arms full of groceries. "Any chance one of you can grab the last bag from the car?"

"I'll get it, Mom," Elizabeth said.

"It's Steven," Jessica grumbled. "Mom, you should hear him going on and on about having ESP! It's not even funny. And he doesn't stop when we ask him to cut it out."

"He'll get sick of it soon," Mrs. Wakefield said lightly, setting the bags down on the table. With her blond hair and bright blue eyes, Mrs. Wakefield looked like a grown-up version of the twins. She worked part-time for an interior design firm in town.

"But we don't want to wait for him to get sick of it," Elizabeth protested, coming back inside with the bag of groceries. "Can't you talk to him about it, Mom?"

"Well . . ." Mrs. Wakefield's eyes twinkled. "I can try. But if I know your brother, he's not going to stop until he gets good and sick of it." She smiled at the twins. "I'm surprised you two haven't already put your heads together and thought of some way to make him stop. You're usually good at that sort of thing."

Jessica's eyes shone. "You're right, Mom!"

She looked long and hard at Elizabeth. "I don't know why we haven't struck back sooner. We've just got to figure out some way to make him hate ESP as much as we do!"

Elizabeth giggled. No doubt about it—things were always exciting when Jessica Wakefield decided it was time to take action!

Elizabeth still had almost an hour before her mother needed her help with dinner, and she decided to ride her bicycle to the library to see if they'd gotten in any new mysteries. She and her best friend, Amy Sutton, both loved to read. They would take turns getting books out from the library, and trade them back and forth.

Mrs. Donaldson, the librarian, gave Elizabeth a knowing smile when she came in.

"We just got the latest Amanda Howard mystery in," she said with a twinkle in her eyes. "Something told me you might be interested in it, so I tucked it away under my desk."

Elizabeth's face lit up. She thanked the librarian before moving away to look at the "new books" shelf in the young readers room. To her surprise, she saw Pamela Jacobson, one of her classmates, sitting in an armchair by the window.

"Hi, Pamela!" Elizabeth said with a friendly smile. "I didn't know you liked coming to the library!"

Pamela was a small, pretty girl with soft brown wavy hair which came down to her shoulders. She had a slightly pale complexion and blue-gray eyes. She looked up with a shy smile from the book she was reading.

"Oh, I come here all the time." she said. "Do you come here often?"

"Yes, but we must come at different times," Elizabeth said as she pulled up a chair. Elizabeth didn't know Pamela very well. Pamela had entered Sweet Valley Middle School in the sixth grade, and Elizabeth still thought of her as a "new girl."

"I love to read," Pamela added. "This book is great. Have you ever heard of Amanda Howard?"

Elizabeth burst out laughing. "She's one of my favorite authors," she confided.

Soon the two girls were discussing their favorite titles. Talk of books led to talk of *The Sweet Valley Sixers* school paper, which Pamela said she would like to write for.

"Our next issue is going to be a special one. We're covering the Mini Olympics Day," Elizabeth told her. "Maybe you can write a feature story about that. Mr. Bowman said it would be good to get more people involved in it." Mr. Bowman, their English teacher, helped Elizabeth organize the paper. He was a nice man, and Elizabeth liked him, though she had to agree with Amy that he was the worst-dressed teacher at the middle school. Sometimes he even wore striped shirts with plaid pants!

Pamela looked pleased. "I'd like to," she said.

"Are you excited about the Mini Olympics?" Elizabeth asked her. "Did they have something like that at your old school?"

Pamela blushed. "I can't really do anything athletic," she said, looking down. "I've got a heart condition. The school I used to go to was for special kids. We didn't have anything at all like the Mini Olympics."

Elizabeth felt like kicking herself. She hadn't known that Pamela's old school was for disabled children, but she should have remembered that Pamela wasn't allowed to participate in gym class.

"It's OK," Pamela said quickly, seeing how uncomfortable Elizabeth was. "Believe me, Elizabeth, I like it when people forget I'm different!" She looked shy. "It's much worse when people remember and make a big fuss. The truth is, I'm fine as long as I don't overdo anything. I mean, I can't run, and I'm not allowed to exert myself very much. But as long as I follow everything my doctor tells me to do, I'm perfectly fine!"

Elizabeth looked at her with admiration. "You have such a good way of looking at it. You seem to want to do everything you can for yourself."

"That's why I left Ridgedale," Pamela told her. "Because everyone there was 'special,' I started to think of myself that way too." She frowned. "Some of my teachers thought I was making a mistake when I said I wanted to try a regular school. They thought I wouldn't be able to keep up—that I'd feel left out."

Again Elizabeth felt terrible for having brought up the Mini Olympics. It seemed just the sort of event that was bound to make Pamela feel excluded.

Pamela appeared to read her mind. "Every once in a while there's bound to be something I can't do," she said softly. "But I don't mind. I just want the chance to show everyone that I'm OK—that I'm just a normal girl after all." Her eyes shone. "The last thing I want is to get special treatment of any sort!"

Elizabeth nodded in understanding. But she couldn't help feeling that the Mini Olympics Day was unfair. It was meant to be a day everyone could be part of. And that meant Pamela Jacobson should be included too.

Two

"I'm really glad Mr. Butler chose you to be in charge of the Mini Olympics," Janet Howell told Jessica the next day.

The girls were all changing into their striped gym shorts in the locker room. A small group of Unicorns had clustered around Jessica and Lila Fowler, including Betsy Gordon, Tamara Chase, and Kimberly Haver—seventh graders whom Jessica particularly wanted to impress. Lila Fowler, a tall, slender girl with auburn hair and a pretty face, was also a Unicorn. She was the only daughter of one of the wealthier men in Sweet Valley. Whatever she'd ever wanted was hers for the asking. Lila had been selected assistant chairman of the Mini Olympics. But from the expression on her face when Janet spoke, it was apparent she wasn't pleased about Jessica having been put in charge ahead of her.

"What sort of events are you planning to add this year?" Lila asked casually.

Jessica had been giving this matter a great deal of thought. She wanted to make the Olympics more competitive. Usually the classes were divided into four equal teams—the Red team, the Blue team, the White team, and the Black team. Points were awarded to each team throughout the day, and at the end of the Mini Olympics one team was declared the victor. "I think we need to have individual trophies this year," Jessica declared. "And we should have more field events, more jumping activities, and a triathlon of some sort."

"That's a great idea," Janet said, her eyes shining. "I'm really proud that the Unicorns have two members working on the committee," she added.

Lila groaned. "Jessica, you just want to add more events that you happen to be good at," she complained. "Everyone knows what a good jumper you are. Shouldn't you be a little fairer to the rest of us?"

Jessica glared at her. "The whole point is to make it a contest," she pointed out. "If it's too easy, where's the challenge?"

Lila didn't look as if this answer satisfied her. "You know, *I* have some really good ideas," she began.

"What's keeping you guys? Ms. Langberg

wants us to start up a volleyball game," Ellen Riteman said, strolling over to the group assembled in front of the lockers. Ms. Langberg was their gym teacher. Ellen was another Unicorn.

Jessica, however, hadn't even noticed Ellen's arrival. She was far too annoyed with Lila. *Why does she always try to steal the spotlight away from me?* thought Jessica. *Isn't it bad enough that she gets a huge allowance and that her father buys her anything she wants if she so much as asks?* Jessica's face was burning. She had to show the others that Lila couldn't get away with criticizing her this way.

"Lila, I think it would be a lot easier for us both if you were behind me," she pointed out.

Lila's eyes flashed. "Behind you! I guess that means just shutting up and letting you do whatever you feel like!"

Ellen put her hand on Lila's arm. "What's going on here?" she asked, disturbed. Ellen liked Lila *and* Jessica, and clearly wanted to end the argument.

"You two shouldn't be arguing," Janet said. "The whole point is that it's wonderful to have *two* Unicorns on the committee." Her face looked dreamy for a moment. "Do you suppose you could have a Purple team this year?"

Everyone laughed. Purple was the Unicorn's favorite color. They used it wherever and whenever they could, and each of the members tried to wear at least one piece of purple clothing each day.

Like the name of their club, it was supposed to signify how special and beautiful they were.

"Janet is right," Tamara chimed in. "You two should be working together. The important thing is to make sure the Unicorns get all the glory, no matter what. Remember?"

Jessica didn't say anything. She couldn't help thinking that she and Lila were fighting about more than just the Mini Olympics. Lila was too spoiled to let Jessica take charge without making things difficult for her, Jessica decided.

But Lila hadn't counted on one thing, Jessica thought with determination: She wasn't going to budge an inch. She had very definite plans about the Mini Olympics, and she fully intended to see them carried out.

Pamela Jacobson took a deep breath as she walked from the locker room into the chilly gymnasium. This was the hour of the day she dreaded most. She bet none of the other girls even thought twice about taking gym class—it must seem like nothing to them!

But for Pamela it was an ordeal.

For as long as she could remember, Pamela had been a special case. It started the minute her parents learned she had been born with a rare heart condition. Pamela was the youngest one in her family, and the only girl. Her two brothers, Sam and Denny, were both perfectly normal. The doctors had explained that Pamela would always have to be careful. She underwent an operation before she was two years old, and another when she was seven. Those operations had saved her life, but they couldn't make her one hundred percent better. Her heart was always going to be weak, and though her doctor believed she would be able to live a full, long life, she still had to live under a shadow. She couldn't do many of the things her friends could do. No running. No strenuous activities. She had to take medication, and above all—and this was the very worst part—she had to put up with her parents' concern.

Pamela's father was a doctor himself, and Pamela sometimes thought that made everything even worse. Dr. Jacobson was the most overprotective father in the world. He was the one who had insisted Pamela go to Ridgedale, the private school twenty miles from Sweet Valley for special-needs students. He treated Pamela as if she were an invalid, even though he knew she wanted to be treated just like her brothers. Dr. Jacobson had been upset when she begged to leave Ridgedale. Only after months of pleading would he listen to her at all—and that was mostly because her mother was on her side.

In the end Dr. Jacobson had backed down. But he had only agreed to let Pamela leave Ridgedale with the understanding that at the slightest sign of fatigue, depression, or any other danger signal, Pamela would have to return to Ridgedale.

It made her cringe just thinking about it. Not that Ridgedale was a bad place. She had made a lot of friends there, and she cried the day she left. It was just that Pamela wanted a chance for a normal life. She wanted to prove—to her father *and* to herself—that she could do it.

But she was finding it wasn't that easy. Little things that no one else even thought twice about were difficult for her. At Ridgedale there were ramps instead of stairs, so that children in wheelchairs could manage on their own. Pamela got tired easily, and even a short flight of stairs had to be taken slowly. Sweet Valley Middle School was almost twice as large as Ridgedale, and that meant the distance between classes was longer—and the time to get from one to the next much shorter. Pamela found herself arriving late to every single class. If she hurried, she'd risk tiring herself—and injuring her heart.

But these problems could be handled. Her teachers understood her condition, and no one objected when she arrived late. The hardest part by far was that Pamela felt left out. Most of the activities she longed to join involved exercise—like the Booster Squad or the gymnastics club. And then there were the Mini Olympics coming up. It hurt Pamela to think of having to sit on the sidelines. At least at Ridgedale she didn't stick out. *Everyone* there had some sort of handicap. But here . . . here there was only Pamela.

She took a deep breath as she decided to go

sit in the bleachers. A fierce volleyball game had already started up. Somehow the Unicorns had all managed to get on the same team. Pamela looked on wistfully. She wondered what it would feel like to be a Unicorn. The girls in the club were all so pretty and confident. She couldn't help feeling a twinge of bitterness as she thought about the name they had chosen for themselves and the reasoning behind it. "We're called Unicorns because unicorns are special, and so are we." She had heard Janet Howell explain it that way to Ken Matthews. Pamela shook her head. She could tell them all a thing or two about being "special." For instance, that being special in a crowd was a lot easier than being special alone.

Tamara Chase suddenly caught sight of Pamela sitting on the sidelines. "Pam, come play with us!" she urged.

Pamela's face turned red. "I can't," she said.

"But we need a ninth person," Tamara pressed her.

Pamela shook her head. "No—really. I'm not allowed to."

Tamara frowned. She didn't say anything, but her message came through to Pamela loud and clear. She could feel tears welling up in her eyes. *I'm such a weakling,* she thought, feeling completely disgusted with herself. The tears spilled over, and Pamela got to her feet. She stumbled blindly to the door of the gymnasium. Why had she chosen to sit in on gym class today? If only she had gone to study hall instead. Maybe her father had been right after all—maybe it had been a mistake to believe she could fit in. She wasn't normal at all. She'd been foolish to believe she could make it through the year.

"Poor Pamela," Elizabeth murmured to Amy. They were in the cafeteria, looking over at the small brunette, who was eating lunch by herself. Elizabeth and Amy were talking about what had happened in gym class that morning. They really sympathized with Pamela. Elizabeth couldn't imagine what it must be like, feeling so shut out from ordinary activities. Turning to Amy, she said, "Let's go over to see her. Maybe I can talk to her again about the newspaper."

Amy nodded enthusiastically, and the two girls hurried across the cafeteria, their trays in hand. Pamela's eyes brightened when she saw them, but Elizabeth could see she had been crying.

"Volleyball," Elizabeth said after a minute, "is probably the world's stupidest game."

"Yeah," Amy added. "I can't stand it. I hate it when Ms. Langberg makes us play."

Pamela wiped a tear from her cheek. "You guys are just trying to cheer me up," she murmured.

Elizabeth giggled. "Who, *us*? Amy, did you just hear what she accused us of doing?"

Amy pretended to cover her ears with her

hands, and in spite of herself Pamela began to smile a little.

"I know it's silly to get so upset," she said softly. "The thing is, I feel like . . . I don't know, like such a wimp! I hate not being able to do what everyone else does."

"It must be really hard," Elizabeth said softly, sitting down beside her. "I think you've got a lot of guts, Pam. You promise you'll let us know if there's ever anything we can do to help you?"

Pamela sighed heavily. "I'm afraid no one can help me with the thing I want," she said. "I want to prove to my father that I can make it here, that I don't need to be in a special school." She looked miserable. "He's already been saying that I look more tired than I did last year, when I was at Ridgedale. And he's upset because I'm left out of so many activities." She bit her lip. "I think he's been trying to convince my mom to have me transferred back to Ridgedale." Pamela shook her head. "And I just want to convince him that I can do it! But I don't know how."

Elizabeth and Amy exchanged glances. The thought of Pamela being sent back to Ridgedale upset them both. Elizabeth decided then and there to talk to Jessica about taking Pamela's case into consideration in planning the Mini Olympics.

"Don't worry, Pam. We'll help you find some way to stay," she said quickly. Elizabeth knew her promise was rash. But she also knew she had to do something to help!

Three

"OK, Liz—now remember the plan," Jessica whispered to her sister. The twins were out in the backyard, by the Wakefields' swimming pool, enjoying the late afternoon sunlight and waiting for their brother to get home from basketball practice so they could try out their scheme.

"I still don't think it's going to work," Elizabeth objected.

Jessica's blue-green eyes were indignant. "Trust me, Lizzie! As soon as we make Steven feel he really *does* have ESP, he's going to be really scared. The only reason he's been going on and on about it is because he thinks it's all a joke."

Elizabeth had planned to talk to her sister about Pamela Jacobson and the Mini Olympics the minute she got home, but she had found Jessica so excited about her plan to get back at Steven that she couldn't get a word in edgewise.

"So remember—make sure that whatever Steven predicts is going to happen really *does* happen," Jessica advised her. "And be sure to egg him on. Ask him all about his 'visions,' and let's pretend to get really scared." She grinned. "As soon as we start to take him seriously, he's going to flip! He'll be sorry he ever said a word about ESP!"

"I bet you guys are glad I'm here," Steven declared a moment later, opening the screen door and coming out to join them. He had a bag of cookies in one hand and a carton of milk in the other, and Elizabeth made a face.

"How you can eat all that junk is beyond me," she muttered.

Steven stared. "I had a premonition today," he announced. "My ESP is getting stronger all the time, you guys. This morning"—he popped a cookie in his mouth—"I had the most amazing feeling that one of you was in trouble." He chewed the cookie solemnly. "It was about ten-thirty," he added.

Jessica poked Elizabeth, her eyes widening with mock horror. "Ten-thirty? Are you serious?" she gasped.

"Yeah," Steven said, surprised by the strength of her reaction. So far no one had paid any attention to any of his "omens." "Why?" he asked. "Was I right? Did something happen to one of you?"

Jessica paused dramatically. "Steven, I didn't believe you up until now, but you really *must* have ESP!" She shuddered. "I was in gym class at ten-thirty, and I just missed getting hit in the head with a volleyball. Ms. Langberg said I could have been hurt really badly."

Steven's eyes widened. "Wow," he said. "That really happened at ten-thirty?"

Jessica nodded energetically. "Cross my heart," she fibbed.

Elizabeth knew the nudge her twin was giving her meant it was her turn. "What about me? Have you had any weird feelings about me lately?" she asked.

Steven thought for a minute. "Well, yeah. I guess I did. This afternoon, during basketball practice, I had this sudden feeling that you . . . uh, that you had just found some money." He looked closely at her. "But I guess ESP isn't right one hundred percent of the time, is it?"

Elizabeth winked at Jessica. "I can't believe it," she said to her brother, feigning astonishment. "You must have overheard Amy Sutton telling someone about the five-dollar bill I found on the way home!"

Steven blinked, looking confused. "How could I have possibly run into Amy? I was at basketball practice, and then I just came straight home."

Elizabeth gave Jessica a look of mock concern. "We thought he was making it all up," she said.

Jessica nodded seriously. "Steve, we owe you an apology. This is incredible—you really do have ESP!"

Steven looked a little alarmed. "Liz, you really found a five dollar bill this afternoon?" he demanded.

Elizabeth nodded solemnly.

Steven looked slightly pale. "Listen, I've got to make a phone call," he said abruptly, getting up from the deck chair and hurrying across the patio toward the back door.

Jessica and Elizabeth exchanged triumphant grins.

"See, I told you," Jessica said happily. "He never really expected we'd start taking him seriously. Now that he thinks he really has ESP, he's scared to death!"

Elizabeth looked thoughtful. Now that her brother was gone, she wanted to turn the conversation to Pamela.

"Jessica, I've been wanting to ask you something about the Mini Olympics," she said. "I know you've been putting a lot of time and effort into the whole thing, and I'm really impressed with some of your ideas. But there's one thing that's been bugging me."

"What's that?" Jessica asked, only half listening as she thumbed through her notebook, looking over the plans she and Mr. Butler had drawn up so far.

"Well, I had a talk with Pamela Jacobson at

lunch," Elizabeth began. "It really made me do some serious thinking. Do you know she isn't allowed to participate in any of the regular gym activities?"

"Mmmm," Jessica said, flipping through pages with a frown. "Yeah, she had to sit out our volleyball game this morning. I don't really see why she came to gym at all today. What's the point? If she's too sick to play, she shouldn't bother coming."

"That's the whole point—she isn't *sick,*" Elizabeth said, defending her. "She's got a heart condition, and that's different. It's never going to go away."

Jessica looked up, her eyes slightly narrowed. "Liz, what does Pam Jacobson have to do with the Mini Olympics? I don't mean to be rude, but I just sort of assumed she wouldn't even show up. What would be the point?"

"There wouldn't be any point—not the way things have been run in the past. Not the way you're planning to run them again this year," Elizabeth said slowly. "The truth is, Jessica, it seems kind of unfair. Why shouldn't someone like Pamela be able to join in?"

Jessica frowned. "She could help decorate posters or something," she mused. "Is she any good at typing? We've got a bunch of flyers we want to send out to parents."

"That wasn't what I meant, Jess," Elizabeth said firmly. "I don't think Pamela wants to *work* for this. I think she'd like the chance to compete—to actually get involved, like everyone else."

"OK," Jessica said. "But I don't think she's going to have much of a shot. Most of the events we've got planned are pretty hard. She's going to have to get in much better shape if she wants to win anything."

Elizabeth looked horrified. "Jessica, she *can't* compete in difficult events! She could really hurt herself!"

Jessica put her notebook down with a frown. "Isn't that what I said in the first place? Come on, Liz. You're not making any sense."

"What I was thinking," Elizabeth said, sitting up straighter, "was making some changes in the events this year. Why not include some races or relays that don't require much strength or speed? What about adding a talent contest in the afternoon, or having a tent with puzzles and games in it? That way some of the smaller kids in the lower school would participate too."

Jessica sighed. "That sounds like a nice idea and everything, Liz, but Mr. Butler and I already put tons of work into the arrangements. You wouldn't believe how much time it's taken. Besides, what's the point of going to all the trouble to rearrange everything when I like it the way it is?"

"It doesn't seem to me like it would take that much work," Elizabeth said. "And I think it would really be worth the extra trouble. Jess, think what it must feel like for Pamela. Here she is, trying to prove she can make it in a normal school, and what does she find—that she isn't allowed to take part in half the things the rest of us do!" She looked intently at her twin. "Try to picture something you do every day that you never think twice about—like climbing the stairs or something."

"Yeah," Jessica said. "I'm picturing it."

"Well, now think about what it would be like if you had to make a really big effort to do it—just to climb the stairs!" Elizabeth exclaimed, upset.

"Listen, I feel sorry for Pamela too," Jessica assured her sister. "But I don't see any way to solve her problem. Who knows," she added, picking up her notebook again. "Maybe it was a mistake for her to try coming to a regular school. Maybe she should have stayed where she was."

"I can't believe you can even say something like that!" Elizabeth cried. "Jessica Wakefield, take that back!"

Jessica looked up at her with surprise. "OK, OK—I take it back," she said quickly. She wasn't used to seeing her sister so upset, and she decided she had better keep things calm. She promised to think over what Elizabeth had suggested.

"I'll talk to Mr. Butler about it," she said. "But I really think it might be too late, Liz."

"As long as you try," said Elizabeth. "That's all I'm asking, Jessica." Her eyes shone. "You're a great sister, you know that? I owe you a favor in return—whatever you want. OK?"

Jessica's face brightened. "Good," she said,

setting her notebook down again for good. "Because I *do* have a favor to ask of you." She leaned forward confidentially. "It has to do with Steven. I've got the perfect plan to finish off what we started this afternoon. With a little luck we should have him so frightened he won't even be able to look at his own shadow without getting the creeps."

Elizabeth sighed. "What have you got in mind this time?" she asked. Knowing Jessica, it could be anything. Elizabeth hoped she hadn't spoken too soon when she'd promised to help her!

"You know, Steven," Jessica said that night at dinner, buttering a piece of bread, "I looked up ESP at the library the other day, and according to the book I found, people who have it sometimes see visions—usually at night."

Steven put down his glass of milk, frowning at her. "Really, I haven't seen anything at night," he said.

"Steven, you've barely eaten a thing!" Mrs. Wakefield exclaimed, looking concerned. Steven's enormous appetite was a big joke in the Wakefield household, and any change was usually a sign that something was seriously wrong.

"I'm just not very hungry," Steven said.

Jessica gave Elizabeth a meaningful look. Their plan seemed to be working. "Maybe you're being affected by the supernatural vibrations," she suggested hopefully. "Maybe that's what's spoiling your appetite."

"Sounds to me like too many chocolate chip cookies after school," Mrs. Wakefield said with a smile.

"Maybe," Jessica said, taking a bite of her hamburger, "you'll see a spirit one of these nights when you're sleeping, Steven. Did you ever think of that?"

Steven was beginning to get angry. "I *don't* see things, Jessica," he muttered. He got up from the table, threw down his napkin, and stormed out of the room.

"What on earth—" Mrs. Wakefield began.

"He's just a little touchy today," Jessica said sweetly. "Liz and I think his ESP is beginning to get to him."

Mr. Wakefield gave Mrs. Wakefield a concerned glance. "I hope he's all right," he said. "You don't think he really *believes* any of this nonsense he's been feeding the girls about ESP, do you?"

Jessica and Elizabeth exchanged glances. Steven might not have believed it to begin with, but with their help, he was obviously starting to get worried.

And after what they had planned for that night, he was never going to consider ESP a joking matter again!

Four

"I still think this is a bad idea," Elizabeth said in a low voice. She and Jessica were out in the garage, using flashlights to find their way in the dark. It was past midnight, and they were trying their hardest not to make any noise. If Mr. or Mrs. Wakefield found out they weren't in bed, they'd get in very bad trouble. Not to mention the fact that they were about to do something really rotten to poor Steven. Elizabeth felt terrible about it. She wished she hadn't promised Jessica a favor.

"Shhh," Jessica said. She almost tripped over a piece of garden hose, and her face went white as she grabbed Elizabeth by the arm. "Darn. It's so hard trying to do this in the dark!"

"Let's forget it," Elizabeth begged her. "Can't we just keep doing what we've been doing?

Steven's already getting spooked. He'll cut out this ESP stuff any day now."

But Jessica had already managed to get the ladder off its hooks on the garage wall. "No way," she whispered back. "We've got to teach him a lesson. Help me with this thing, Lizzie. It weighs a ton."

The twins had to struggle with the ladder before they got it safely out of the garage. It was heavier than they'd expected, and so it was no easy chore to carry it over to the side of the house where Steven's bedroom was located. Jessica took the ladder from her sister and opened it up against the side of the house. "That's perfect," she whispered. "Now, stay right here while I go back for my ghost costume."

Elizabeth shook her head and frowned, but before she could say a word, Jessica was running back to the garage in the dark, her flashlight making a bright bouncing mark as she ran. It was chilly out, and Elizabeth shivered.

It seemed ages before Jessica came back, holding a white sheet in her hand. It was left over from a Halloween party. "Remember—pass it up to me once I'm up at the top," Jessica whispered as she started to climb the ladder.

"I really think we should go back inside," Elizabeth said again, this time more firmly. "Jess, what if we really scare him? He could get hysterical or something!"

"You promised to help out," Jessica reminded her. "Don't worry," she added. "He may be scared for a second, but then he'll probably just laugh. And he'll *definitely* get the idea. Then we won't have to hear any more about ESP!"

Elizabeth laughed. "I guess he does deserve it," she admitted. "Remember the time he scared you in that ridiculous Creature from the Black Lagoon costume of his?"

On Halloween night Steven had tormented Jessica by sneaking into her room in the dark and giving her the shock of her life. The more Elizabeth thought about it, the more she had to admit that Steven deserved a taste of his own medicine.

"I remember," Jessica said grimly. "He"ll be sorry for that—and for this ESP nonsense!" Soon she had climbed up to the top. The ladder was wobbling quite a bit, and Elizabeth began to feel nervous.

"Careful!" she warned, steadying the ladder with both hands.

Jessica reached down. "Give me the costume," she instructed.

Elizabeth passed it up to her, watching anxiously as Jessica balanced on the top of the ladder, holding onto the window ledge as she draped the sheet over herself. There were two holes cut in the sheet for the eyes, and Elizabeth thought Jessica really did look scary. It was strange how different everything looked out here in the pitch dark. She watched as Jessica inched closer to the window and tapped at the glass.

"I don't think he can hear me," Jessica said a minute later. "I'm going to try pressing my face against the glass."

Meanwhile Steven was sitting up straight in his bed, his heart pounding. What was that sound—that scratching at the window? He thought about what Jessica had said that night at dinner. Was it really true that people with ESP had visions? His face went pale. He'd never really believed he had ESP. He only told his sisters that to have some fun. Now he wished he'd never brought it up.

Taking a deep breath, he threw off the covers and padded over to the window. The shade was pulled down. He felt a terrible chill when he heard it again—a faint but definite knocking on the glass. The next moment he snapped up the shade and screamed as loud as he could when he saw—he didn't know what it was—something white and terrible pressing against the window. It was just inches from his own face!

"Jessica!" Elizabeth cried. She didn't know what had happened, but when the shade snapped up, Jessica started, and her left foot slid off the top rung of the ladder. The next instant she was clawing desperately at the sill, but it was too late for her to regain her balance. With a bloodcurdling scream she crashed down, pulling the ladder over with her. "Jessica," Elizabeth cried again, trying to pull the sheet off of her. "Jess, are you OK?"

Lights were being turned on all over the upstairs as Steven's and Jessica's cries woke Mr. and Mrs. Wakefield. By now Steven had yanked open his window and stuck his head outside. "What's going on down there?" he demanded, his color returning to normal as he realized that what he had seen wasn't a vision at all.

"Steven, get Mom and Dad—quick!" Elizabeth cried. "Jessica's hurt!"

"Jessica—" Steven choked out. "Why, that little . . ." His anger settled down as the meaning of Elizabeth's words finally struck him. "Is she OK? I'll be right down!" he cried.

"Don't tell them," Jessica moaned, trying to pull herself up. "Liz, they're going to *kill* us!"

"Are you all right?" Elizabeth demanded, leaning over her with concern. "Gosh, Jess—I thought you'd killed yourself!"

"So did I," Jessica grumbled. "Liz, try and help me up. I think I hurt my ankle."

Elizabeth gave Jessica her arm, but Jessica couldn't pull herself to her feet. "Something's really wrong, Liz," she groaned, leaning over and clutching her ankle. "I think I broke it!"

Elizabeth peered unhappily down at her sister's leg. "You must have caught it in the rung when you fell," she said sorrowfully.

"Jessica! Are you all right?" Steven hollered,

racing toward them around the side of the house. Mr. and Mrs. Wakefield weren't far behind.

"What on earth is going on here?" Mr. Wakefield said angrily. The ladder was lying on the grass, and Jessica—her face stained with tears—was sitting shivering beside it, the sheet still wound partially around her.

"The ladder fell," Jessica whispered.

"Jessica's hurt," Elizabeth said quickly, shining the flashlight toward Jessica's leg. "Look—her ankle's starting to swell up!"

"She's not really hurt that bad," Steven said, looking disgusted. "Jessica, what do you think you were doing? I thought you were"—he swallowed—"a *burglar* or something."

Jessica looked up fearfully at her parents' stormy expressions. "We were just trying to scare him a little," she whispered. "We were pretending I was a spirit." She gulped. "We were sick of him acting like he had ESP."

Mr. Wakefield knelt down on the grass, expertly gripping Jessica's ankle. "Tell me when it hurts," he said, putting a slight pressure on the bone.

"Ouch!" Jessica cried.

"I think," Mr. Wakefield said, getting up with a frown, "that you and I had better make a trip over to the Emergency Room, Jessica. We'll talk tomorrow morning about what you two girls were up to and why. For now, I think we had better get a doctor's opinion about that ankle."

Jessica looked pale as her father picked her up in his arms. She knew she and Elizabeth were in trouble. But she was even more upset about her ankle. It hurt so badly it took all she had not to cry.

She couldn't believe her bad luck. She just had to hope against hope that it wasn't broken!

"Well," Dr. Lawrence said, coming out to the waiting room of the hospital, where Jessica and her father had been waiting for half an hour. "We've got the X-rays. You're lucky, Jessica. It's just a bad sprain."

Jessica let out a long sigh of relief. "That's great," she said. "I've got so much to do in the next few weeks! I don't know what I would've done if it was broken."

"Well," the doctor said, frowning down at the X-rays, "I hate to disappoint you, but you're going to find day-to-day activities a little difficult for the next couple of weeks anyway."

"What do you mean?" asked Jessica.

"Well, you've got quite a nasty sprain," Dr. Lawrence told her. "Most people don't realize it, but a bad sprain can be more painful than a break—and take almost as long to heal. You're not going to be able to put any weight on your left ankle for at least three weeks."

Jessica's eyes widened. "How am I going to get around? You mean I can't even walk on it?"

"That's right." Dr. Lawrence smiled. A look of horror washed over Jessica's face. "I wouldn't be so upset. You'll be able to use crutches, so you won't be confined to your bed or anything that drastic." He wrote something down on a piece of paper and handed it to Mr. Wakefield. "I'm prescribing this for pain," he said. "She should keep these to a minimum—one or two every four hours, as needed, for the first few days." He turned back to Jessica. "You'll have to keep the Ace bandage wrapped tightly around your ankle all the time, except when you're taking a bath. When you're sitting down, I want you to keep your leg elevated. And under no circumstances put any weight on it at all!"

Jessica bit her lip. "But I'm in charge of the Mini Olympics," she said sorrowfully, "and I'm cheering with the Boosters at the game on Monday, and—"

"No, you're not," Mr. Wakefield said. "First thing tomorrow morning I'll go out and get you a pair of crutches so you can get to school." He shook the doctor's hand. "Thank you very much for all your help," he said. "I think this young lady learned a lesson tonight. Haven't you, Jessica?"

"I guess so," Jessica mumbled. She looked down at her ankle with hatred. How in the world could she have been so clumsy? This was all she needed. She had more going on in the next few weeks than she could ever remember, and she wasn't even going to be able to walk normally!

Even worse, she knew that she was about to face her parents' anger—not to mention Steven's.

She had a feeling Elizabeth wasn't going to be too happy with her either.

All in all the little scheme she had cooked up to scare her brother had really backfired! She didn't know which was worse—the prospect of getting yelled at by her parents, or the terrible throbbing in her ankle.

She couldn't even get up from the chair by herself. Her father had to carry her out to the car like she was some kind of invalid!

"I'm not going to go through a whole lot of nonsense about what you and Elizabeth tried to do to Steven tonight," Mr. Wakefield said when they were alone. He put the key in the ignition and frowned. "I think you've learned your lesson. And if you haven't yet, I think you will." He started the car's engine. "I sprained my ankle when I was about your age, and I seem to remember that by the time it was better, I had made up my mind never to goof around again. Anyway, the sprain was punishment enough. And I think it will be for you too."

Jessica felt a little bit better. She thought her father was being extremely soft on her. True, her ankle was throbbing. But it was only a sprain. How bad could it be? So she'd have to use crutches for a few weeks. That couldn't be *that* bad.

No, she had definitely gotten off lightly. She couldn't wait to get home and brag about it to Elizabeth.

Five

"Jessica! What happened to you!" Caroline Pearce shrieked, making her way through the crowd surrounding Jessica in homeroom. Mrs. Wyler, their teacher, was trying to remind the class about the chocolate bars they were selling to raise money for the class trip at the end of the year. But no one was paying attention. They were too interested in Jessica's injury.

"You poor thing," Caroline gushed. Caroline, a redheaded girl with a sprinkling of freckles across the bridge of her nose, was a real gossip, and lived two doors away from the Wakefields. She loved knowing exactly what was going on with everyone, and Jessica could tell she was upset she hadn't been the first to hear about her ankle.

"It's no big deal," she said airily. "Just a sprained ankle."

But the truth was, it had been a hard morning. Everything that Jessica usually did took at least twice as long. Getting downstairs for breakfast was an ordeal, let alone managing to carry her books while she used her crutches. Still, it wasn't so bad. In a way it was even kind of fun. For one thing, she had never gotten so much attention. Everyone came up to her in the hall, wanting to know what had happened. Bruce Patman had carried her books for her from her locker to her homeroom—and he usually didn't even say hello! Bruce was a seventh grader—a really cute, dark-haired boy whose family was the wealthiest in Sweet Valley.

Only one thing was making her unhappy, and that was Steven. He couldn't believe she and Elizabeth weren't being grounded after what they'd done. He didn't believe his father's explanation that Jessica's injury would be punishment enough for her. As far as Steven was concerned, nothing was punishment enough! So he was refusing to talk to her. He had somehow come to the conclusion that Jessica was really to blame, not Elizabeth—so he was still talking to Elizabeth. It wasn't fair.

But Jessica was determined to put Steven out of her mind. She didn't want to dwell on the mishaps of the night before either. She was just going to bask in all the attention she was getting.

Lila came hurrying into homeroom. "Jessica! I heard you sprained your ankle," she said, sounding sympathetic. "I just couldn't believe it! But it seems to be true," she added, looking down at Jessica's Ace bandage. She made little clucking noises, shaking her auburn head. "I guess you won't be able to be chairman of the Mini Olympics anymore," she said after a minute.

Jessica's face burned. So that was why Lila was being so nice! "Why not?" she demanded. "It's only a little sprain, Lila. It's not really a big deal, and it certainly isn't going to affect my thinking!"

Lila looked taken aback. "Oh. Well, if you need any help . . ." she began.

But Jessica didn't even want to talk to Lila about it. Luckily, Mrs. Wyler interrupted the conversation by ringing a small bell on her desk. Homeroom really had to get under way—so Jessica, using her crutches, made her way over to her desk.

She noticed Pamela Jacobson giving her a sympathetic smile as she tried to arrange the crutches next to her desk. Finally she had to lean them against the window and hop back to her desk.

She didn't like what Pam's smile seemed to mean. After all, there wasn't anything really wrong with her—this was just a temporary thing.

It wasn't as if she and Pamela had anything in common!

"Steven still isn't talking to me," Jessica said

glumly. She and Ellen Riteman were eating lunch together. It was Thursday afternoon, two days since Jessica's accident, and Jessica had to admit having a sprained ankle wasn't very much fun anymore. In the first place, people weren't paying as much attention to her as they had the day before. Now that everyone had tried her crutches and heard all about the accident, they seemed to have forgotten about it.

"You seem kind of down in the dumps," Ellen said.

"Well, having a sprained ankle today isn't half as much fun as it was yesterday," Jessica complained. "It's getting to be a real pain. Everything I do takes twice as long. I can't even get up or down stairs without it taking practically forever!"

"That's too bad," Ellen said sympathetically.

"I can't even ride my bike," Jessica said mournfully. "I can't do anything anymore!" She stuck her lower lip out. "And no one's even paying any attention to me. I don't think anyone even cares about my ankle—besides you, Ellen," she added hastily. She knew she was complaining, but she couldn't help it. Things suddenly seemed extremely gloomy.

Cheering with the Boosters, of course, was out. Jessica couldn't practice, so she sat on the sidelines and watched, feeling left out. They were supposed to be learning a new cheer that week, too, and she was sure she'd never get the hang of it by the time her ankle was better.

Then there were the Mini Olympics. Jessica had devoted so much time to planning them, and now she could barely make it to the meetings on time, let alone control them! It was infuriating. And Lila Fowler really seemed to be taking advantage of her predicament. She kept insisting that Jessica allow her to do more work, now that she was injured. If Mr. Butler had anything special he needed done, Lila begged him to let her do it—since, as she kept saying, it would take so much effort for poor Jessica on crutches. It was clear that Lila was trying to take over her job, and Jessica couldn't stand it.

"You don't seem very happy," Ellen said. "I guess it isn't much fun having to hobble around all the time."

"I'm not hobbling!" Jessica protested, putting down her sandwich. She'd lost her appetite. "I guess I'm getting a little tired of it," she admitted. "There are so many things I feel like doing, and it's no fun being left out."

"I know," Ellen said feelingly.

But Jessica wasn't sure she *did* know. Ellen had never been left out of anything! Until that week Jessica hadn't been either.

She didn't like it. Not one little bit.

"Today is it," Ms. Langberg said, after she had blown her whistle and gotten everyone's attention. "And I mean it! This is the final volleyball game, and I want you girls to give it all you've got."

Jessica sighed. She was sitting on the bleachers, watching the Unicorns giggling and patting each other on the back as they faced the net. She couldn't stand it. Here it was, Friday. Another long day dragging around on crutches. She'd do anything to be out there with Janet, Lila, and the others.

"Hi, Jessica," a familiar voice said. Pamela Jacobson had come over and was standing next to her. "Mind if I join you?" she asked timidly.

"No, go ahead," Jessica said with a sigh.

"Not much fun, is it?" Pamela said. She sat down, and the two girls watched the volleyball game in silence. "This is what I hate the most," Pamela said after a while. "I don't think there's anything in the world as bad as having to sit on the sidelines."

Jessica looked up at her thoughtfully. She hadn't known that Pamela wanted to be part of things so badly. "I guess you're right," she said.

"Of course," Pamela added, as if she were reading Jessica's mind, "it's probably worse for you. I mean, I've *always* been this way. It must be a lot harder if you're used to being in the middle of everything."

Jessica pretended to look at her fingernails. She didn't like to admit it, but it occurred to her—for the first time—that she had never really considered what it must feel like for Pamela. She shrugged. "I don't think so," she said. "I think it must be harder for you. I mean, I've only got to put up with this dumb ankle for the next couple of weeks."

Pamela thought this over. "Yeah," she said finally. "Maybe you're right."

The two sat together in silence for a while, watching the volleyball game. Jessica kept thinking how different it all looked from the sidelines. Everyone seemed to be having such a good time!

"Sometimes," Pamela said, "I think I should just give up and go back to Ridgedale."

Jessica forgot that she had said almost the same thing to Elizabeth just a few days earlier. She looked at Pamela with horror now. "Don't say that," she said. "I'm sure things will change around here—once everyone gets used to your condition. Things will get easier."

Pamela shook her head. "The thing that really gets to me is that at Ridgedale I was an outsider too—because I was so much better off than most of the kids! They resented me a little." She sighed. "I guess I hoped I'd finally feel like I belonged once I got to Sweet Valley."

Jessica didn't know what to say. She couldn't help feeling relieved that her own injury was temporary. Things seemed really rough for Pamela.

"Come on, Steven," Jessica begged, trying hard to keep up with him on her crutches. They were in front of the school, and Steven was definitely not interested in slowing down to listen to what she had to say.

"How many times do I have to say I'm sorry?" she cried.

Steven turned to glare at her. "Sorry isn't good enough this time," he snapped. "How would you like it if I tried to scare *you* to death?"

Jessica felt exhausted all of a sudden. The crutches were beginning to hurt her underneath her arms. She was also sick and tired of begging Steven to forgive her. "If you weren't such a big baby, you wouldn't have been scared. You wouldn't have screamed, and I never would have fallen off the ladder," she retorted.

Steven's face darkened with anger. "That just isn't true," he growled. "It was all your fault, and you know it!" He looked as if he were about to say something more, but instead he turned away and hurried off across the parking lot.

Taking a deep breath, Jessica tried to decide what to do for the next fifteen minutes before her meeting with Mr. Butler, Lila Fowler, and the rest of the Mini Olympics committee began. Then she remembered something.

Because of her ankle, it would probably take her fifteen whole minutes just to get to the gym and get herself ready for the meeting!

Six

The meeting wasn't going the way Jessica had planned at all. There were six people in the room: Mr. Butler, a woman named Ms. Ulrich from the PTA, Jessica, Lila, and the two fifth graders who were working with them on the Mini Olympics—Randy Osborne and Patty DuVal. Randy was a cute, dark-haired boy with a good sense of humor, and seemed to be devoting a lot of time and effort to his role organizing the four teams. Patty was in charge of publicity. Jessica considered her a really nice girl who had always listened to her in the past.

But this afternoon Jessica felt like she shouldn't have made the effort to show up. No one was listening to anything she said! At first she thought it was her imagination. She was trying to make a suggestion about the first event they had scheduled—the long jump. Jessica wanted it to be moved around so that they began with water races in the lower school pool. "It seems to make more sense to start off inside, and then move outside for the rest of the day," she said.

Lila cleared her throat. "Don't you remember, Jessica? We've already taken care of that. We're having three parts—first the pool and water events, then the sand pit for long jump and high jump, and then the field for races and relays." She gave Mr. Butler a smile so sweet that Jessica thought she was going to get sick. "Isn't that what we said, Mr. Butler?"

Mr. Butler nodded. "Yes, that's right," he said.

Jessica couldn't believe her ears. "When did you talk about it?" she asked, her voice a little unsteady. "I thought we had decided on Tuesday that—"

"Lila got in touch with me yesterday and said you two had decided this order would be better," Mr. Butler said, frowning. "Isn't that right, Lila? I was under the impression that you two had discussed it already."

Ms. Ulrich patted her hair and cleared her throat. "I'm sorry, but I have another meeting in less than half an hour. If we could just firm up these plans . . ."

"No problem, Ms. Ulrich," Mr. Butler said, frowning at Jessica. "We'll move through the rest of the events as quickly as we can."

Jessica stared at Lila. She couldn't believe it. What a sneak! Obviously Lila had been using Jessica's injury as a chance to move in on her role as chairman. Jessica decided it was time for immediate action.

"Can I just ask Patty how the publicity is going?" she asked. "We weren't sure on Tuesday whether or not to advertise the day at all, and I was wondering—"

"Oh, I took care of all that," Lila said airily. "I asked Daddy to ask some of the people at his advertising agency to run a full-page ad in the *Sweet Valley News*."

Jessica stared at her, her eyes wide with disbelief. She knew Mr. Fowler was rich and powerful, but she couldn't imagine that he'd buy his daughter a full-page newspaper ad! And she couldn't believe Lila was showing her up this way either.

"I thought I was supposed to decide that," she protested.

Mr. Butler frowned at his watch. "Jessica, Lila was just trying to be helpful. It's obvious that it's harder for you to get around now that you've hurt your ankle, and she was just trying to be a friend, that's all."

Jessica bit her lip, trying as hard as she could to control her temper. She couldn't stand the little smirk on Lila's face, though. She had to figure out a way to regain control of the Mini Olympics—no matter what!

The only question was how to do it!

"Boy, you sure don't look happy," Elizabeth said when she saw the look on her sister's face. "Is your ankle hurting a lot?"

Jessica glared at the Ace bandage wrapped firmly around her ankle. "It hurts, all right. But that's not what's bothering me."

"Is it Steven? I know he's been really mad, but he's bound to forgive you sooner or later." Elizabeth patted her twin on the shoulder. "I'll even talk to him if you want me to."

Jessica shook her head. "If Steve wants to give me the silent treatment, let him! That isn't what's bothering me either. It's Lila. She's stealing the whole Mini Olympics right out from under me!"

"What do you mean?" Elizabeth asked, surprised.

Jessica's lower lip trembled a little, the way it did when she was really upset. "It isn't fair! She's just using the fact that I'm hurt to try to take over the whole committee. She keeps coming up with all these suggestions, and if I object to any of them, it makes me look bad. I mean, here I am, injured. And Lila is perfectly ready and willing to do all sorts of things I can't do." Jessica's face turned red. "I just wish she weren't quite so ready to take over everything."

"Maybe she thinks she can do a better job running things than you can," said Elizabeth. "I mean, now that you can't compete in the actual events anymore yourself."

Jessica stared at her. "I'd forgotten about

that," she murmured. "I'm not going to be able to even *be* in the Mini Olympics!"

"Well, I'm sure Lila hasn't forgotten it," Elizabeth said, watching closely for her twin's reaction. "She probably just thinks that she'll have to take over eventually and she might as well do it now. After all," Elizabeth said matter-of-factly, "the Mini Olympics have been planned to exclude certain kinds of people. And I'm not just talking about someone like you or Pamela Jacobson."

"What do you mean?" Jessica demanded. "Who else is being excluded?"

"Well, what about some of the really little kids, and the smaller fifth graders?" Elizabeth asked. "In the past they've always been divided equally among the four teams. But wouldn't it be better if instead of seeing them as handicap points, they got to participate in events where they had a chance of winning?"

Jessica shrugged. "I don't know. Anyway, I still can't think of a single event where any one of them would stand a chance against someone like Jerry McAllister," Jessica said, naming one of the biggest boys in the sixth grade.

Elizabeth laughed. "You're just not using any imagination," she teased her sister. There was a silence for a minute before Elizabeth began pressing her point further. "Then," she said slowly, "there are the older kids who just aren't any good at sports. Think about Lois Waller, for instance."

Jessica made a face. "*You* think about Lois

Waller," she said. Lois, clumsy and overweight, was in the sixth grade. Jessica and the Unicorns loved to make fun of her. "Lois is just lazy," Jessica added. "She *needs* exercise, Lizzie! Are you suggesting we plan the Mini Olympics so that every single weakling has the same chance to win that some big strong athlete has?"

Elizabeth laughed. "That's exactly what I'm saying," she said. "Only you put it much better than I could have."

Jessica shook her head. "Only you would consider remaking the Mini Olympics so that Lois Waller and Pamela Jacobson could win blue ribbons, Liz. It's a nice idea and everything, only I just don't see how—"

"And," Elizabeth cut in, "of course *you'd* get all the credit for thinking of it, wouldn't you?"

Jessica stared. "What do you mean?" she demanded.

Elizabeth shrugged. "Just that it sounds like Lila Fowler is being her usual pushy self, that's all. And she probably doesn't realize how insensitive she's being either. If you gave Mr. Butler and Ms. Ulrich a new plan—one that would include *everyone* and make the Mini Olympics totally fair—Lila would end up looking like a rat."

Jessica's eyes shone. "She would, wouldn't she!" she cried. "She barged in without one tiny bit of sympathy for me. She hasn't even asked if I'm still planning to try to be in any of the events.

She's just assuming she can edge me out and be rid of me!"

Elizabeth nodded. "So," she finished casually, pretending not to know the exact effect her words were having on her sister, "a few casual remarks to Mr. Butler now would really solve two of your problems, wouldn't it? First, if you changed the Olympics, you'd be able to take part after all. And second, you'd get control over the whole day back again."

Jessica shook her head in admiration. "Did I ever tell you you're the smartest twin in the whole world?" she cried. "Lizzie, get me my crutches, OK?"

Elizabeth handed her the crutches. "Going somewhere?" she demanded, a curious smile on her face.

"I'm going to call Mr. Butler," Jessica declared. "Elizabeth Wakefield, you're a genius! I'm going to try and convince him that we need to start planning from scratch."

"Good," Elizabeth said sweetly, watching her sister struggle with her crutches as she made her way down the hall to the telephone. She couldn't believe how easy it had been to persuade her sister. She couldn't wait until Jessica was off the phone so she could call Pamela Jacobson and tell her the news.

Pamela's voice sounded funny when she

came to the phone—almost as if she'd been crying. "Oh, hi, Liz," she said, not sounding very excited.

"Are you OK? You don't sound like yourself," Elizabeth said.

"We've been having a big talk here," Pamela said in a low voice. "My dad came home early from the hospital. He thought I'd been going to clubs or over to friends' houses in the afternoons. I guess he's really upset that I'm not getting out more." She sighed. "In fact, he and my mom are downstairs now, talking about it. They don't sound very happy either."

Elizabeth felt terribly sorry for Pamela. "Listen, I called because I think Jessica is trying to do something about the Mini Olympics to change the events. If it works, everyone will be able to participate—including you!"

Pamela's voice sounded dull. "That sounds nice, Liz," she said flatly. "Listen, I have to get off the phone now, OK? My dad wants to talk to me."

"OK," Elizabeth said, concerned. A second later she heard a click as Pamela put the receiver back on the hook. She wished there was something more she could have done or said to give Pamela support. It didn't sound like Pamela was having a very easy time explaining things to her parents.

Elizabeth just hoped that the new plans for the Olympics didn't come too late to prove to Dr. Jacobson that Pamela had a real chance to fit in at

Sweet Valley Middle School. She couldn't bear to think that the Jacobsons were giving up so soon.

Elizabeth was sure that given the chance, Pamela could really prove herself.

All she needed was that chance. And Elizabeth was going to fight as hard as she could to see that she got it!

Seven

Pamela had been dreading this moment for ages. She had suspected for some time now that her father was losing patience with her attending Sweet Valley Middle School. He'd been so bitterly opposed to it from the start that the slightest hitch was all he needed to decide that she ought to go back to Ridgedale.

To her surprise, her brothers were sitting in the living room with her parents when she came home that afternoon. Sam, her oldest brother, was a sophomore at Sweet Valley High. He had curly dark hair and a friendly expression that drew people to him naturally. The look he gave Pamela when she entered the room told her he was on her side.

But Pamela knew Denny felt differently. Denny was in the eighth grade, and he had taken his father's side when the family began to discuss where Pamela would go to school. Denny joined every club there was and excelled in every sport. Pamela was ashamed of herself for feeling this way, but sometimes she suspected that he was a little embarrassed to have her in the middle school with him. She knew she wasn't the kind of sister he would have liked to have. He probably would have liked someone like Jessica Wakefield: Someone who was a Unicorn, and in the Boosters. Not a wimp like Pamela, who had to get an excuse to be late to every class because she walked so slowly!

"Pamela," said Dr. Jacobson. "We've been talking about the Mini Olympics your class is putting on for the lower school next Friday. Why didn't you mention it to us? If it hadn't been for Denny, we never would have known about it!"

Pamela blushed. "I . . . uh, I guess I was just waiting to tell you about it when it got a little closer," she said faintly.

Mrs. Jacobson's dark eyes looked concerned. "Honey, we're not trying to grill you. Your father was just afraid that you'd been excluded from it, that's all."

Pamela's eyes burned with tears. Bad as it was being left out of things, it was a million times worse having to tell her family every time it happened.

"The Olympics are really athletic," she said, swallowing hard over the lump in her throat. "I've been thinking about trying to get involved in other ways—like working on the special edition of the class newspaper."

Dr. Jacobson looked at her with a sad frown on his face. "Pamela, we don't want to put you on the spot. It's not your fault that you can't participate. We're only trying to learn more about what life has been like for you at the middle school so we can come to a rational decision about what's best for you."

Rational, Pamela thought miserably. Her father always used that word. Maybe it was because he was a doctor, and he thought the best approach was to find out what was wrong and then think of the most reasonable way to fix the problem. She knew deep down that it probably wasn't *rational* to want to stay at Sweet Valley Middle School so badly. At Ridgedale she got so much more attention. There were only eight or ten students in each class. At Ridgedale she didn't have to take any risks. She could finish middle school at Ridgedale and go on to Parker Academy, the high school for disabled students. That way she would never have to feel hurt and embarrassed about trying to do things that were too hard for her.

But that wasn't what Pamela wanted. She *wanted* to take a risk. She wanted to prove she could do something difficult, that for once she didn't need to have things cushioned and protected for her. Pamela had always longed to be treated the way Denny was treated. No one ever gave him a break. They expected things from him, and he lived up to expectations. He got good grades, he had lots of friends, he was good at games. *Denny* had won three blue ribbons at the Mini Olympics the year he was in the sixth grade!

"Your father is afraid you're isolated from people at school," Mrs. Jacobson said, putting her arm around Pamela. "He's afraid you haven't really been meeting very many people. But you're making friends, aren't you?"

"Yes," Pamela said. "I am."

"Why aren't they coming over to the house?" Dr. Jacobson asked. When Pamela's face fell, he added, "I'm really not trying to hurt you, honey. I just want to find out a little more about what your life has been like there. Can't you tell me?"

Pamela sighed. "I guess things are moving kind of slowly," she admitted. "But I'm shy too. It's not easy being in a new school. It never is!"

"Pamela," her father said softly, "how much time do you think you ought to give it? We want to be supportive of you. But we don't want to see you get hurt."

"We said a year!" Pamela cried, anguished. "You promised I could stay for all of sixth grade."

"But we didn't know what it was going to be like then—any of us," her father reminded her. "I'm just wondering whether you still want to stay all year or whether you'd like to consider going back to Ridgedale sooner. Maybe next month."

Pamela's lower lip began to tremble. "I want to stay," she whispered. Her mother hugged her, sympathetic tears welling up in her eyes.

Denny looked disgusted. "You're making a big mistake," he declared. He jumped up and ran out of the room.

"Denny's wrong," Pamela said miserably. "I think I've got a chance at school! It's just going to take a little time."

No one said anything, and after a minute Pamela couldn't bear the silence. She got up from the couch and went into the hallway and to her bedroom, which was on the first floor off the foyer.

She closed the door, tears streaming down her face. She had a lot of thinking to do. And she really needed to be alone.

Pamela was so unhappy she could barely concentrate on the Amanda Howard mystery she was reading in the big, comfortable chair in the reading room of the town library. Her eyes kept filling with tears, and the words looked blurry on the page.

"Amanda Howard!" Elizabeth Wakefield said in surprise. "Twice in a single week! You and I must have ESP."

Pamela made an effort to smile, but Elizabeth could tell at once something was seriously wrong.

"Are you OK?" she asked. She pulled a chair over to join Pamela.

Pamela swallowed. "I guess," she said dully. "I've been thinking so hard all day, and everything seems so confused. My father wants me to go back to Ridgedale next month," she concluded.

Elizabeth's heart sank. "You've got to talk him out of it," she said. "Pamela, I know you can make everything work out!"

Pamela shook her head. "I don't think so," she said. "Maybe my father's right. What's the point of trying to stay at Sweet Valley when things are only going to get harder and harder? I don't belong in a normal school, Elizabeth. I belong with people like me. I need special help and special attention." She shook her head, knowing that she was only saying the things her father always said. She sounded as if she had memorized his words.

"I don't believe that," Elizabeth declared. "You just need to keep trying, Pamela. Don't you think that it's important that people in so-called normal schools find out more about so-called special students?"

"What do you mean?" Pamela asked.

"I mean," Elizabeth said, "that the way things are run now at school, all sorts of people are excluded. Unless you're really pretty, or really good at sports, or really smart, no one notices you. And most people aren't any of those things. Think of all the kids you know at school who are bad at sports, and imagine how much they suffer through things like gym class or the Mini Olympics."

Pamela looked thoughtful. "I guess I hadn't really thought about that," she mused. "I know it's been hard for your sister since she sprained her ankle. Is that what you mean?"

Elizabeth shook her head. "Jessica's ankle will be better in a few weeks. I'm thinking more about people like Lois Waller, who are just naturally bad athletes. Or Jimmy Underwood." Jimmy was one of the smallest boys in the sixth grade, and though he was good at schoolwork, he was always chosen last for teams.

Pamela didn't look convinced. "It's one thing to be bad at sports; it's another to be handicapped. I can't even *try* at Sweet Valley Middle School. And I think my father's right. I don't think it's a very healthy place for me. I need to be with people who are like me."

Elizabeth got the feeling nothing she could say was going to change Pamela's mind. But she felt terrible about the decision Pamela had made. And she could hardly wait to get home and find Jessica. If Jessica was going to try and change the format of the Mini Olympics, she was going to have to hurry.

It seemed to be the only chance to change Pamela Jacobson's mind.

"OK, OK," Jessica said, holding the edge of the kitchen counter as she hopped over to the sink. "I can't wait till this stupid ankle gets better," she added, filling a glass with water and taking a sip. "Now tell me again. Pamela's having fits because of the Mini Olympics, so she's planning to drop out of school and go back to Ridgedale."

"Her father wants her to go back as soon as possible," Elizabeth said gloomily. "I feel terrible for her, Jessica. I think you should get her involved in the new Olympics committee."

Jessica looked thoughtful as she sipped the water. "That's not a bad idea," she murmured. "I could probably even make a stronger case if I brought Pamela in with me. That way Mr. Butler and Ms. Ulrich would feel really sorry for her. And they'd be way too embarrassed to say we shouldn't consider her feelings if she's standing right there!"

"You'd better be careful," Elizabeth warned. "Pamela's very sensitive."

"I know that," Jessica said. "Pamela and I have been spending a lot of time together, remember? We sit next to each other on the sidelines in gym."

"Well, I think it's a great idea," Elizabeth said. "When are you supposed to meet with the committee?"

"I called Mr. Butler and asked him if we could hold an emergency meeting tonight. The Mini Olympics are only a week away, and if we're going to change the plans, we've got to get going."

"Good," Elizabeth said. "And I'm going to talk to Mr. Bowman and see if he can help me to get Pamela to work on the special edition of *The*

Sweet Valley Sixers." She pulled her blond hair back from her face with both hands, the way she often did when she was thinking hard about something important. "I think if we can get Pamela involved in things, maybe she'll forget all about Ridgedale."

Jessica didn't comment. She didn't really care where Pamela Jacobson went to school. She just wanted to make sure that she got back control of the Mini Olympics . . . and that she made Lila Fowler realize once and for all who was really in charge!

Eight

Half an hour later Jessica was ringing the door bell of the Jacobsons' house. She hoped she'd be able to get Pamela to come to the meeting with her. It had been so difficult getting over there! There was nothing like a sprained ankle to make getting around a real pain in the neck, she thought ruefully.

At last a tall, dark-haired man whom Jessica assumed must be Pamela's father came to the door. "Hello," he said, looking surprised.

"My name is Jessica Wakefield," Jessica said politely. "Is Pamela home?"

"She's in her room. I'll go call her," Dr. Jacobson said. He looked at her ankle. "I'll bet that hurts," he added. He looked pleased that she had come by to visit.

Jessica nodded. Her eyes brightened as she

caught sight of Denny Jacobson in the front hall. "Hi, Denny," she said warmly, getting into the house with an effort. Denny was one of the cutest boys in the eighth grade, and Jessica, who loved to flirt, suddenly realized there might be advantages to spending more time with Pamela.

Denny smiled at her. "How'd you hurt your ankle?" he asked her.

Jessica didn't think he'd want to hear about the real story, so she decided to tell a white lie. "I fell trying to learn a new Boosters cheer," she said. She knew Denny loved the Boosters.

Unfortunately, Pamela came out just then, so her conversation with Denny was interrupted. "Hi, Jessica," she said, looking even more surprised to see her than Dr. Jacobson. She gave her father a little glance, as if to say, "See? People *do* come by to see me!"

"Pamela, I've come to talk to you about the Mini Olympics," Jessica said, not noticing the startled expression on Denny's face. "Can we sit down somewhere and talk? I really need your advice."

"Sure," Pamela said, wide-eyed. "I don't know what advice I can possibly give you, but I'd be happy to help in any way I can."

Soon Jessica was sitting on the flowered bedspread in Pamela's room. She looked around her, suppressing a sigh. Everything was so tidy—it was as bad as Elizabeth's bedroom! No posters of rock stars, no jumble of clothing on the floor—nothing to make it look comfortable and lived-in, like Jessica's own bedroom. Still, she hadn't come over to inspect the Jacobsons' house. She didn't have much time, and she'd have to go to work on Pamela right away.

"Has Elizabeth talked to you about the Olympics being unfair?" Jessica asked, getting right to the point.

"A little," Pamela said. "But I don't really see what can be done about it. Contests are always unfair. If they were *fair,* they wouldn't be fun."

Jessica frowned. "I don't know about that. Sure, we need to have competition. But doesn't it seem like the events should test different kinds of skills, instead of being all sports? The way Lila has things planned now, people like you—and me—are left out in the cold."

"I didn't know Lila was the one who wanted it that way," Pamela said, surprised.

Jessica looked at her sadly. "It's hard to believe, isn't it? She seems so nice and everything. Believe me, Pam, I've done everything I could to get the committee to be more open-minded." She lowered her voice confidentially. "Just between you and me, it's reaching the point where I think Lila and I are going to have some kind of showdown."

"Wow," Pamela said, her eyes wide.

"But I need your help," Jessica added. "First

of all, I don't know much about special kinds of races and stuff. I figure you guys must have had things like Special Olympics at Ridgedale, right?"

Pamela nodded. "Sure. We had wheelchair races and a whole bunch of contests that anyone could do. You know, things involving brainpower more than strength."

"That's exactly what I was thinking of!" Jessica cried. "We could even have a race where everyone had to use crutches," she added slyly. Jessica was sure by next Friday she'd be good enough on crutches to beat anyone in the sixth grade.

"But do you really think the committee wants to change the Mini Olympics?" Pamela asked. "I thought everyone was happy with things as they were."

"Oh, I guess some people were," Jessica said, ignoring the fact that before she'd sprained her ankle she had been more than happy with the events that had been planned. "But it doesn't matter if people are *happy* with the events, Pamela. People need to learn. They need to realize that not everyone can throw or run really fast or climb ropes." She was getting warmed up to this idea now, forgetting she had taken it from Elizabeth.

"You're really amazing, Jessica," Pamela said, looking excited. "If you can pull this off, and convince them to let you make some changes—"

"Of course I can pull it off!" Jessica declared. She gave Pamela a quick look. "I mean, *we* can pull it off," she amended. "Pamela, I think Mr. Butler and Ms. Ulrich will be much more likely to think about the changes I suggest if you come along with me to the meeting tonight. We have to make them see just how unfair they've been. Will you do it? Will you come with me?"

Pamela thought it over. "I don't see why not," she said. "It sounds like a really good idea, Jessica. If I can help, at least I'll have done *one* useful thing before I leave Sweet Valley Middle School."

Jessica got to her feet with an effort, reaching for her crutches. "Do you think your mom and dad could give us a ride to school? That's where we're supposed to meet the others."

Pamela nodded. "I'm sure one of them can," she said.

"Then let's go," Jessica cried. "I'm sure between the two of us we can convince them to do exactly what we want!"

And in the meantime we can make sure Lila Fowler comes out looking like a real creep, she thought happily. If that wasn't killing two birds with one stone, then what was?

"Well," Mr. Butler said, taking off his glasses and looking at Jessica and Pamela with a frown. "I have to admit you two are pretty convincing. Jessica, why didn't you bring any of this up earlier?"

"I was afraid to," Jessica said. She looked pointedly at Lila. "I was afraid some of the others wouldn't approve."

Lila's pretty face was pinched with anger. "I suppose you mean *me,*" she snapped.

"Lila, please," Ms. Ulrich said. "It seems to me that Jessica and Pamela have a very legitimate point of view. One that we really should consider carefully." She frowned at Lila. "I don't see what good it can do to argue about it."

"But the whole thing is planned," Lila wailed. "We've put so much time into everything, and it's only a week away!"

Jessica cleared her throat. "I used to feel just the way Lila does," she said, shaking her head. "I kept thinking that once we'd gotten the plans under way, it was too late to make any changes. Then I realized that I was just being lazy. I was doing what people always do when they really know—deep down—that things could be changed, but they don't want to go to the trouble of doing anything about it."

"Hear, hear!" Ms. Ulrich cried, striking the side of her chair with the rolled-up copy of the plans for the Mini Olympics.

Lila's face was positively stormy. "Before you sprained your ankle you weren't worried about people with 'special needs,'" she accused Jessica. "I think you just want to make sure *you* still get to be involved!"

"Lila," Mr. Butler said reprovingly, "you can't really mean that—"

"No, Mr. Butler," Jessica said generously, "Lila is partly right. Until I sprained my ankle I didn't realize what it's like trying to do simple things in a world made for people who don't need crutches or wheelchairs. Just one week of trying to get around like this has made me realize how unfair our whole world is." She shook her head, beginning to throw herself into the dramatics of the speech now. Soon she had given a lengthy description of the ways in which handicapped people were treated with prejudice by the rest of so-called normal people. Her performance was so stirring that even Mr. Butler began to look misty-eyed. Only Lila continued to glare at her.

"Well, Jessica, as far as I'm concerned, you have my permission to make any changes you think appropriate," Mr. Butler said. "What do you think, Ms. Ulrich?"

Ms. Ulrich was clasping her hands, beaming. "I think these two girls deserve special recognition," she declared. "Jessica Wakefield, I'm going to see that you get the PTA Civic Service Award! You are an amazing young woman, and you truly deserve a commendation."

Lila pouted, her lower lip sticking out, the whole time Pamela and Jessica arranged with Mr. Butler to meet the next day to begin rethinking the Mini Olympics. She waited until the adults had left the room before telling Jessica what she thought.

"You're a rotten creep," she said furiously. "You knew I was doing a great job getting things in shape! Why did you have to butt in?"

"Lila," Jessica said reprovingly, "you're making it sound like I have *selfish* reasons for wanting these changes. Remember what Ms. Ulrich said. It's the good of the whole school that Pamela and I are thinking of. Isn't that right, Pamela?"

"Right," Pamela said, glancing at the plans for the Mini Olympics with a frown. She wasn't very interested in the argument Lila and Jessica seemed to be having. She was much more interested in the replanning of the Mini Olympics.

In fact, she could hardly wait to begin.

"Steven," Jessica called from the kitchen. "I know you're giving me the silent treatment, but could you come out here and help me carry this? I can't carry a snack and use my crutches at the same time."

"I'm through with not talking to you, anyway," Steven said, coming into the kitchen and taking the bowl of popcorn from her. He popped several pieces into his mouth. "I've been having premonitions again," he added smugly. "Something tells me you've been up to trouble."

"I thought you were through with ESP," Jessica grumbled, following him into the family room.

"It's back. Can I help it?" Steven said.

Jessica decided the best thing to do was to ignore him. Instead of discussing his ESP, she told him about the meeting that evening and the changes she and Pamela were going to make in the Mini Olympics.

"My ESP tells me this has something to do with your ankle," Steven said dryly. "Like the fact that you want to make sure you've still got a shot at winning some events, right?"

Jessica gave him a cold look. "That isn't right at all," she told him. "For your information, Ms. Ulrich happens to think I should get the Civic Service Award from the PTA this year."

Steven groaned. "Civic service, my foot," he said sarcastically. "The only service you care about is Jessica Wakefield service. You couldn't be more selfish if you tried!"

"Be quiet," Jessica snapped. "You don't know anything about it."

Personally, she liked the thought of winning an award for caring so much about others. She thought it was an appropriate end to a long, hard task. And she couldn't wait to get started working on the Mini Olympics again and show Lila Fowler what *real* leadership was all about!

Nine

Jessica could scarcely believe it was four-thirty already. The day had flown by. It was Sunday, and she and Pamela had been hard at work down in the Jacobsons' basement since noon. Papers were strewn all around them, and next to Jessica was a stack of notebooks—records of previous Mini Olympics she had borrowed from Mr. Butler.

"It's really weird that no one ever objected to the way the events have been organized before," Jessica said, thumbing through the records from several years earlier. "You'd think—in all this time—someone else would have come up with some changes like this."

Pamela shook her head. "People don't like change," she said. "That's one reason it's so hard for those of us who just don't fit in. We've got an extra hard time of it—first, convincing people that we even exist. And second, making them want to do something about it."

"Well," Jessica said, "I think you and I are going to go down in Sweet Valley Middle School history, Pamela." She couldn't help thinking secretly that *she* would probably get all the credit. As it was, everyone at school thought she was a saint for helping Pamela. At first, when the news broke that Jessica had convinced Mr. Butler and Ms. Ulrich to let her reorganize the whole day, no one could believe it. But within hours it was all over school. Jessica had decided it was unfair not to have events *everyone* could take part in. The way she and Pamela were going to make it, even little kids—and bad athletes—were going to have a chance.

All through the following day people stopped Jessica in the hallways. Everyone wanted to know when she'd gotten the idea, how she'd ever found the courage to approach Mr. Butler about it, whether it was true she and Lila weren't getting along anymore, and if her sprained ankle had anything to do with the change in the Olympics. Jessica adopted a new humble pose. After all, she was soon to be a famous Good Citizen. She merely smiled graciously, tossed her hair, and admitted she had always thought sports events were unfair. It was just time to do something about it, that was all.

"You're such a natural leader, Jessica," Caroline Pearce said admiringly Friday morning in homeroom. "Maybe you should run for Student Council."

The elections were coming up, and Jessica couldn't help agreeing that Caroline might have a point. Granted, she had never been interested in student government. Elizabeth had been talking about running for treasurer, and Jessica had already told her that she couldn't imagine anything duller than sitting around for hours arguing about things with faculty representatives. Not when she could be having fun with the Boosters, or shopping at the mall! But now she saw things differently. It was fun being the center of attention. *Maybe it wouldn't be so bad running for office after all. Jessica Wakefield, first woman president of the United States,* she thought dreamily, riffling through the pages of the old records.

"I think you're doing a terrific job," Pamela said loyally. Her eyes looked a little moist. "Jessica, I'm so lucky to know you and your sister. School has been so much more fun these past few days!" And her father had noticed the improvement, too, she thought. He had already mentioned several times how glad he was that Jessica had been coming by so often.

Jessica felt alarmed. It was one thing standing up for her and rearranging the Olympics on her behalf—especially since Jessica got to reap most of the benefits. But she certainly didn't want Pamela getting the wrong idea. She seemed like a nice enough girl, but Jessica had always been *very* choosy about her friends. Not like Elizabeth, who seemed to be drawn to serious types like Amy Sutton. Jessica just hoped Pamela didn't start following her around all the time, expecting to be asked to be a Unicorn or something.

But Pamela didn't seem the type, and Jessica relaxed as they turned back to their work. She liked being over at the Jacobsons' house, especially when Denny was around. "Your brother is cute," she told Pamela as they began to put together the master list of new events. "Does he like anyone at school?"

Pamela shook her head. "He doesn't like girls. Especially not me," she confided.

Jessica thought that was too bad. She had been secretly hoping he would notice her, especially since she'd been coming around to the Jacobsons' house so much. Maybe he'd change his mind about girls when he got to know her better. "Janet Howell and Ellen Riteman are coming over to my house tonight," Jessica told Pamela. "I'm going to show them the plans we've made. Do you want to come?"

Pamela shook her head. "No, but thanks for asking me. I promised my father I'd stay in tonight. He thinks I'm overexerting myself."

"OK," Jessica said, gathering her things together. *Just as well,* she thought. This way she could be sure she got all the credit for the long hours she and Pamela had put in these past few days.

"I didn't know you were coming over too," Jessica said to Lila. She couldn't believe Lila could wear the kind of clothes she did. She looked straight out of *Seventeen* magazine in a suede skirt and boots.

"I'm *sorry,*" Lila said coldly, sweeping into the house.

"Let's go up to my room," Jessica said quickly, catching sight of her brother. She didn't want Steven to start having his "ESP" in front of her friends.

"See, we've completely reorganized everything," Jessica said proudly once her door was closed and they were all out of Steven's earshot. "We're still going to have four teams. But no one will be allowed to sign up for a specific event. Say you have someone like Winston Egbert on your team, who you know is a good runner. You can't sign him up for the three-legged race. The way it'll work is this: at the start of each event a representative from each of the teams will draw a slip of paper out of a hat. Each team member has a number. If your number is called, you're in that event. That way it's completely fair—everyone has an equal shot at the event."

"But if you're good at sports, won't you still have an advantage?" Janet demanded.

Jessica shook her head. "We've changed the events so only some of them require physical strength or speed. We're going to have a lot of events that just require brainpower. Puzzle solving, for example. In one event two people from each team will be tied up, and they'll have to untie themselves. We're going to have a bed-making competition—who can make a bed the fastest, including hospital corners. And an egg race. The water events are all going to be changed too. In one you have to use a kickboard to balance a bowl of water, and whoever knocks the least amount of water out wins."

Lila frowned. "It sounds ridiculous," she said. "Who ever heard of a bed-making contest in a Mini Olympics?"

"There are lots of things like that," Jessica said calmly. "Dr. Jacobson is getting us four wheelchairs from the hospital, and we're going to have wheelchair races." She grinned. "We're even going to have an event called Crutch Croquet. A croquet field will be set up, but the contestants have to use crutches—one to walk with, and one to hit the balls."

Lila groaned. "And I suppose you're just going to magically draw the right number so you'll get to be in that event, right?"

Jessica pretended to look hurt. "I don't understand you, Lila," she said. "I'm trying my hardest to change things so it'll be a fun day for everyone, and you're not being a very good sport."

"Good sport!" Lila looked furious. "How can I be a good sport when you're just changing everything so you can still participate?"

"That isn't true," Jessica said hotly. "I happen

to be thinking about Pamela—and other people like her."

"Come on, you two," Ellen said uneasily.

"You should have seen Jessica buttering up Mr. Butler and Ms. Ulrich," Lila complained. "It was sickening! I knew she was only thinking about herself the whole time, and here Ms. Ulrich practically wants to make her a saint. It was awful."

Jessica's eyes flashed. "Lila, you've been really rotten about this whole thing from the minute you were made the assistant chairman! You're not being one bit supportive. I think I've had a good idea, and I'd appreciate it if you'd stand behind me, instead of trying to make me look selfish all the time."

"I can't help it," Lila grumbled. "I want the Olympics to be just like they were last year—and the year before."

Jessica was about to snap back when she saw the expression on Janet's face and stopped. Janet was Lila's cousin, after all. It was hard to tell how they really felt about each other, but Jessica certainly didn't want to hurt her position with the Unicorns. Maybe she'd better not make her feelings so obvious.

Anyway, she knew she had the support of Mr. Butler and Ms. Ulrich. That was all that mattered. It was pretty obvious that Janet and Ellen both thought her ideas were great, and the PTA was going to give her a special commendation for good citizenship. As long as she didn't tell Lila off in front of Janet, it looked to Jessica as if she had emerged from this whole thing a clear victor.

And Lila would be sorry when she saw how well it all came off this Friday. Jessica was sure of that.

"Jessica?" Mrs. Wakefield said, coming into her bedroom. It was nine-thirty, and Jessica was just turning to her math homework. She was tired from the events of the day, but she knew she had to get this done or she'd be in trouble in school.

"What is it, Mom?"

"Your father and I have been talking," Mrs. Wakefield said. "We just wanted to let you know how proud we both are of you. I think what you've done this week takes real courage. It would have been a lot easier just to let things stand as they were. Instead you were willing to make waves. And I think what you've done will make a real difference—not just this year, but in the future too."

Jessica couldn't believe her ears. Her mother never talked to her this way!

"We've been saying as much to your brother and sister too," Mrs. Wakefield said with a smile. "We told both Steven and Elizabeth how proud we feel of you. And I'm sure they feel just the same too."

Jessica couldn't believe her ears. *Boy, Steven must've loved hearing how generous and caring I am!*

she thought. But she didn't have long to wait before she heard her brother and sister's reaction.

"I can't believe what a snow job you've done," Steven said a few minutes later, when Mrs. Wakefield had gone back downstairs. He and Elizabeth came into Jessica's room looking indignant. "You've sure fooled them! I told them that I'm having the strongest signal ever from my ESP—that the minute your ankle is better you're going to forget all about the handicapped. But they didn't believe me."

"Thanks, Steven," Jessica said dryly. "Nothing like a big brother's vote of confidence, that's what I always say." She gave Elizabeth an injured look. "You don't believe me, either, do you?"

Elizabeth didn't know what to say. She wished she believed that Jessica had suddenly turned so good-willed, but she couldn't help thinking there was a grain of truth in what her brother said.

Anyway, Jessica's ankle was getting stronger. She had a feeling they'd find out before too long what the true story behind Jessica's new outlook on things really was.

Ten

"Do you really think you're going to have time to write a story about the changes you and Jessica have made in the Mini Olympics?" Elizabeth asked Pamela. The two girls were sitting together in the library at school. Elizabeth had been explaining the way *The Sweet Valley Sixers* worked. Mr. Bowman would want a final draft of the story by Thursday afternoon so it would be ready for Friday's special edition of the paper.

Pamela looked thoughtful. "I've never written this kind of thing before, but I think I can do it. You know, Elizabeth, isn't it weird how one thing leads to another?"

"What do you mean?" Elizabeth asked curiously.

"Well, I thought about trying to write something for the paper before, but I guess I felt . . . I don't know. It was as if I didn't want to try, because I felt so hurt about being excluded from the things I really *did* want to do. Like the Boosters." Pamela smiled shyly at Elizabeth. "I don't think the kids at Sweet Valley Middle School are the only ones who need to learn about being handicapped, Elizabeth. I think *I* need to learn a little bit myself."

Elizabeth looked surprised. "But . . . what can you possibly have to learn?" she asked her.

Pamela looked as if she were trying to think of the best way to phrase what she wanted to say. "I don't think I've made things terribly easy since I started school here," she admitted. "It's easy enough to put all the blame on my father. And it's true that my dad has been against my attending a normal school from the start. But I think I made things harder too. I had such high expectations!"

"Like what?" Elizabeth demanded.

"Like . . . I don't know, like thinking people were going to come to *me,* asking me to join things, trying to make friends." She shrugged. "I guess I felt special when I came here and I expected people to treat me differently from everyone else. And that's silly. The truth is, I didn't try all that hard to get involved in the things where my handicap wouldn't matter. You tried to get me involved in the paper about half a dozen times," she reminded Elizabeth.

Elizabeth nodded. "That's true. I was beginning to think you just weren't interested."

Pamela shook her head. "But I am interested! I guess it's taken me a while to see that *I'm* the one who has to make sure I fit in here. You and Jessica have really helped me to see that, Elizabeth." She smiled. "Anyway, I'm thrilled to be able to write up what we've done. I don't know how good a job it's going to be, but I can certainly try my best!"

"That's great news," Elizabeth declared. "I don't know about you, Pam, but all this talk about the Mini Olympics is really getting me excited. I can hardly wait for Friday!"

"Me too," Pamela said happily. And from the way her eyes were shining, Elizabeth knew that she was telling the truth.

"What are we going to *do* about him?" Jessica demanded glumly, coming into her sister's room and slamming the door shut behind her. "Liz, I just don't think I can stand it anymore. Steven is driving me crazy!"

"Why? What's he doing now?" Elizabeth asked, looking up from the magazine she was reading.

"He claims he's got a psychic *hunch* about which team is going to win tomorrow. And he's threatening to make a lot of money out of it by setting up bets and charging people for his 'ESP' tips on how to place them."

"At least he's using his business sense," Elizabeth said cheerfully. "Oh, Jess, I wouldn't worry about it," she added, seeing how glum her sister looked. "I'm sure he'll get sick of all this psychic stuff before long."

"Yeah, well, I'm sure sick of it," Jessica muttered. "I don't think I can stand another minute of it, to tell you the truth."

"Is it my imagination," Elizabeth said, "or are you feeling a little bit . . . how should I put it . . . funny?"

Jessica sighed. "Liz, I can't tell you how hard it is, being a famous good citizen. Do you realize Ms. Ulrich actually wants me to go to a lunch with the PTA, to accept this dumb award?"

"Well, that doesn't sound so bad," Elizabeth said. "I would've thought you'd like all the attention—seeing as you're such a famous good citizen and all," she added.

Jessica set her crutches down and wriggled her ankle experimentally. "I think it's getting better," she announced. "It doesn't hurt so much anymore. I can't wait to get rid of these crutches!"

"I still don't see why you mind about the awards lunch," Elizabeth said, closing the magazine and giving Jessica her undivided attention. "You're glad about the way the Olympics have been changed, aren't you?"

"Well, I guess so," Jessica sighed. "I'm just sick of being *good*, that's all." She leaned forward confidentially. "What would you say if I told you the only reason I wanted to change it in the first place was because I couldn't stand being left out?"

Elizabeth pretended to think this over and react with utter horror. "I would never believe it," she declared. "Not in a million years. Not a supremely good citizen like you, Jessica Wakefield!"

Jessica frowned, getting back on her feet with an effort. "It's boring, being a good citizen," she announced, stabilizing herself on her crutches and making her way to the door. "I wouldn't be surprised if I got sick of it pretty soon after the Olympics end," she added.

Elizabeth hid a smile and turned back to her magazine. She wouldn't be surprised either. In fact, the only thing surprising Elizabeth right then was that Jessica had managed to remain a good citizen even for this long!

"Mom," Pamela said shyly, coming into her parents' bedroom. "Can I talk to you for a second?"

"Of course, sweetie," her mother said, looking up at her with a smile. "What's up? Are you excited about the big day tomorrow?"

Pamela nodded. "I really can't wait. It's so nice of Daddy to have gotten us the wheelchairs," she added. She toyed with a hair ribbon, wishing she knew how to say what she wanted to say.

"Are you worried about school?" her mother asked gently.

Pamela nodded, her eyes shining with tears. "I'm starting to like Sweet Valley Middle School," she confessed. "Mom, do you think Daddy might let me stay for the whole year? I really feel like things are starting to get better."

"Oh, Pamela!" her mother exclaimed, hurrying over to engulf her in a warm hug. "Honey, it's really *your* decision. You know your father and I only want what's best for you. If you decide to stay at the middle school, we'll support you one hundred percent."

"But what do you think the right decision is?" Pamela asked anxiously. "I don't want to make a stupid mistake."

Her mother frowned, shaking her head. "I'm not sure I can answer that, Pam. I think you're the only one who knows for sure. I know that it meant a lot to you to try a regular school for a while. And at the same time I've gotten the impression that you've been lonely sometimes. Do you ever miss Ridgedale?"

Pamela thought very hard. "Ridgedale was comfortable," she said at last. "I knew everyone. I knew all the rules. Everyone knew the things I wasn't supposed to do, and there weren't any risks. But . . . I don't know, it wasn't very challenging. I like having to try," she concluded helplessly.

Mrs. Jacobson hugged her again. "I admire you for that," she murmured. "You're a real fighter, honey. You always have been. The doctors say that's what saved your life the two times you had operations on your heart." She held Pamela away for a minute, inspecting her with misty eyes.

"Who knows? Maybe you're fighting for your life in a way this time too. And your father and I never knew it."

"Oh, Mom," Pamela said, throwing her arms around her and feeling tears flow down her cheeks. "I want to stay at Sweet Valley Middle School," she said at last. "I want to try my hardest and see if I can make it."

"Pamela, if anyone can, then you can," her mother told her, her own eyes wet. They were both quiet for a minute, obviously thinking the same thing. "There's still your father to talk to," Mrs. Jacobson said.

The two of them sighed at the thought.

"Maybe tomorrow will help convince him," Pamela said hopefully. "He's coming to the Mini Olympics, isn't he?"

Mrs. Jacobson nodded. "I hope you're right," she said at last. "I don't know why he's been so stubborn about your leaving Ridgedale!"

Pamela didn't know either. She just hoped her father really would leave the decision up to her. Especially now that she felt she knew—for the very first time—where she wanted to be.

Eleven

Jessica couldn't believe it was finally Friday—*the* day. Her worries about being a good citizen completely disappeared as she finished getting dressed, tying a purple ribbon around her ponytail so the Unicorns would know she was remembering them. She was getting a ride from Pamela's mother to the lower school, where the festival was being held. She had to admit Pamela had been a lot of help over the last week. Pamela had lots of good suggestions, and was really good at organizing things. Lila, of course, had been nothing but trouble ever since the Olympics had been changed. But then, Jessica expected as much.

By nine-thirty everyone had arrived at the lower school playground, where team assignments were being made. Mr. Butler read names off from the computer printout made the day before.

The classes had all been divided into four teams. Jessica and Pamela were both on the Blue team. Elizabeth was on the Black team; Ellen Riteman was on the White team; Lila, Janet, and Ken Matthews were all on the Red team. Amy Sutton shrieked with joy when she found out she was on the same team as Elizabeth. Finally the activities got under way. Mr. Butler was the head referee, and he announced the opening events.

The day was divided into three parts. First, there was a talent competition. Each team had to write a song and make up a short skit. These would be judged by Ms. Ulrich and other members of the PTA before lunch. Next, there would be an hour of Brainpower. Tents stocked with games were set up in the fields. There were puzzles, word games, spelling bees, a Password competition, and a junior version of Wheel of Fortune.

Then the final part of the competition would begin. This last phase would involve many of the events Pamela and Jessica had thought up—the wheelchair races, Crutch Croquet, the three-legged race, egg-balancing, pool events, among others.

Jessica was banking on being a contestant in Crutch Croquet. She thought she'd win hands down. Not wanting to leave it to chance, she had already convinced Mr. Butler to let *her* take care of drawing the numbers for her team. After all, she was the chairman. And if she just happened to choose her own number for Crutch Croquet, who would possibly object? Wasn't she a good citizen? No one would accuse a good citizen of rigging the drawing for Crutch Croquet!

The talent part of the Mini Olympics went extremely well. Parents had been invited to come for the whole day and were sitting on the bleachers surrounding the lower school baseball diamond, where each team would perform its skit and song. Jessica thought the Blue team had it all wrapped up. Their skit was called "The Butler Did It" and made fun of Mr. Butler's lower school volleyball coaching. And their song, "The Blue Team Blues," was really catchy. Pamela wrote the lyrics:

Haven't you heard the news?
We've got the Blue Team Blues.
You wake up in the morning and you're
feeling out of sorts; you don't like
dancing and you're tired of sports . . .
What are you going to do?
What are you going to choose?
You know what you've got,
You've got the Blue Team Blues.

None of the other teams came close. The Red team had a really silly skit, which Jessica suspected Lila had made up because it was mostly making fun of a bed-making contest and really didn't make any sense. Their song was silly too. It was called "Dread the Red" and sounded like a Booster cheer. The Black team was pretty good—

their skit definitely showed Elizabeth's touch, as it was all about news reporters trying to find out who was winning the Mini Olympics. Their song, "Black Magic," was cute, with a nice rhyme on "tragic" and "magic." The White team was the worst. Jessica felt embarrassed for them. A fifth grader did a stand-up comic routine instead of a skit, and their song was really a chant without any of the rhymes in the right places.

Jessica and Pamela were practically delirious when Mr. Butler announced that the Blue team had won first place in the talent competition. That gave them one hundred points. The Black team came in second, with ninety points; the Red team came in third, with eighty; and the poor White team trailed with seventy.

"I'll bet you're feeling pretty proud of yourself," Lila hissed to Jessica as they went in for lunch.

Jessica could barely hide a smile. She knew her team was going to win—she just knew it!

After lunch the competition really got serious. Jessica was heartbroken when the Red team won the Brainpower section. The Blues came in third, the Whites came in second, and the Blacks lost—making the score 170 for the Reds and Blues, and the Whites and Blacks tied with 160 points each. It was looking like a much closer race than anyone had expected. The third set of events was going to prove crucial.

Everyone was getting very excited. Parents were cheering loudly, and so were teachers. Jessica could hardly wait for Crutch Croquet. She just knew she could win first place for her team.

The first event of the ten scheduled races was the bed-making contest. To Jessica's joy, Lila was chosen as the entrant for the Red team. She was pitted against Patty DuVal from the White team, Caroline Pearce from the Blue team, and Elizabeth from the Black team. Four mattresses were set up under the flagpole. Each entrant was given a set of sheets, and when Mr. Butler called "Go!" each raced to make her bed. Jessica screamed "Go, Caroline!" so loudly that her throat hurt. Pamela was waving her arms with excitement. Caroline came in second, after Elizabeth. But Lila—and the Red team—had placed last! Jessica was secretly overjoyed. She knew she would never forget the blistering look Lila gave her as she tromped off the field, still holding her top sheet in her hands.

"I'm not surprised you won," Jessica said to her sister. "You get enough practice at home." Elizabeth always made her bed neatly, whereas for Jessica it was at best a once-a-week activity.

The next two races took place in the pool. The first was the kickboard-and-bowl-of-water race Jessica had described to Ellen and Janet. This time the Red team won. The Red and the Blue teams were really neck and neck. The Blue team, however, won the third event. This race was Pamela's idea.

Called the Water Walk, it required that each contestant get in the water and walk across the shallow end of the pool, balancing an egg on a spoon at the same time. Whoever got to the other end first, without dropping the egg, won.

The fourth event was called Untie Yourself. Two entrants from each team were chosen, tied together with twine, and timed as they tried to free themselves. The Red team managed a close win, though their members caused a great deal of laughter—one was tiny Sally Strong, a fifth grader, and the other was Aaron Dallas, one of the biggest sixth graders. The spectators seemed to especially enjoy this event.

Next came the three-legged race, the water-balloon throw, and Pineapple Bowling. Only two events were left: the wheelchair race and Crutch Croquet. Crutch Croquet was the next event, and to her delight Jessica drew her own number out of the hat. "Wow—isn't that weird," she said loudly. "I drew myself!"

"What a coincidence," Lila said in a scathing voice.

"You're just mad because we're beating you," Jessica said.

"You are not. We're ahead by two points," Lila snapped.

"Well, you won't be for long. I'm going to cream you," Jessica said, hurrying off on her crutches to the starting point for the race.

She had to admit she had a real advantage.

None of the other four contestants was used to crutches, whereas she was a real pro. She had raced around the course in less than ten minutes, knocking the croquet ball expertly with her crutch. She wondered if anyone could tell she'd been practicing. In any case, the Blue team won the croquet game easily. The second-place ribbon went to a member of the Red team named Kady Johnson. Lila looked fit to be tied.

"OK," Mr. Butler said, putting his hand up. "We've come to the very last event of the day. Let me just read the scores aloud so you all know where you stand. The Red team and the Blue team are tied for first place—they each have two hundred fifty points. In third place we have the Black team, with two hundred ten points. And in last place the White team, with two hundred points. Now, the final event is a very special event. Each contestant has to steer a wheelchair down the course, and whoever wins this one determines who wins the entire Mini Olympics. Are you all sure you understand?"

Everyone understood. Wild cheers accompanied the drawing of each name. The Red team went crazy when Ken Matthews was called. He was small, but a really good athlete; they were sure now they were going to win. The Black team drew Timmy Peterson, a skinny, sweet-faced lower schooler; the White team drew a fifth grader named Lisa Geiger; and the Blue team drew Pamela Jacobson. A hush seemed to fall across the whole field.

"Good luck," Jessica said solemnly to Pamela, shaking her hand.

"Aw, we've got it all wrapped up," Ken Matthews said in disgust. "It isn't fair—letting me take on two little kids and a . . ." He looked at Pamela, then away again.

"It's OK," Pamela said evenly. "I don't think it's unfair, Ken." She winked at Jessica. "In fact, I wouldn't get overconfident if I were you." She walked over to her wheelchair and sat down, giving Mr. Butler a big smile.

"And they're off!" Mr. Butler called a minute later. The crowd went into a screaming frenzy as they cheered on the four contestants.

Racing in a wheelchair proved to be much harder than anyone could have guessed. Pamela was ahead of Ken by about a foot; and Jessica was screaming "Go, Pam!" so loudly, she thought she'd never be able to talk normally again. Someone else was yelling louder than she was, though. It was Dr. Jacobson. He was cheering so loudly from the bleachers, the whole field seemed to reverberate.

Suddenly it looked as if Ken was closing in on Pamela. He was! He was closer . . . right up next to her . . . and then passing her. Jessica's heart pounded. Ken was inching past Pamela, inching past her . . . and then it happened! He caught his hand in the spokes, lost his momentum, and fell behind as his wheelchair veered to the right. The crowd went wild. Pamela crossed the finish line first. She had won the race *and* the Mini Olympics for the Blue team!

The frenzy that accompanied Mr. Butler's whistle was unbelievable. It was impossible to tell who was hugging whom. Everyone was jumping up and down and shouting, and Jessica thought her ribs would break as her teammates surrounded her.

She knew she had to give special thanks to Pamela, and she made her way through the crowd. Dr. Jacobson lifted Pamela up on his shoulders. He was beaming, and next to him, Denny was patting Pamela's leg over and over again, saying "Way to go. I knew you could do it all along!"

Jessica hoped she wasn't all sweaty from Crutch Croquet. Denny was *so* cute.

"Pamela, you were wonderful!" she said, smiling up at her.

Pamela's eyes were shining. "Wasn't it fun, Jessica? Thank you so much for letting me show I could do it. Daddy, tell Jessica what you just told me."

Dr. Jacobson grinned. "I guess I got a little bit of an education today too," he said to Jessica. "When I saw Pamela out there I realized I'd been trying too hard to protect her." He shook his head. Especially when it's obvious she can take perfectly good care of herself."

"Daddy says I can stay at Sweet Valley!" Pamela told Jessica, her smile glowing.

"That's great," Jessica said, shifting a little on her crutches. "I've got to go now," she added, catching sight of Ms. Ulrich talking to Mr. Butler.

She was sure they were talking about what a model citizen she was. And she supposed she would just have to go over and let them tell her what a great job she had done!

All in all, it had been a wonderful day. And Jessica knew it had meant a lot to Pamela too. The best thing, Jessica thought, was that everything had turned out just the way it was supposed to.

Namely, that Lila Fowler and her team had lost. And Jessica Wakefield had gotten all the glory!

Twelve

"Look!" Jessica exclaimed triumphantly, walking into the sunny kitchen and displaying her empty hands. "No crutches!"

Steven and Elizabeth were eating pancakes. It was Saturday morning, over a week since the Mini Olympics. Elizabeth's eyes widened. "I can't believe it," she said. "Doesn't it hurt to put weight on it?"

Jessica looked scornful. "Not much. It was only a little sprain," she added, opening the refrigerator and studying the contents.

"*Only* a little sprain?" Steven mimicked. "Here we've heard about nothing else for weeks. Didn't I tell you, Liz? The minute her ankle gets better she forgets all about being handicapped."

Jessica made a face, still inspecting the refrigerator's contents. "Don't be a baby, Steven. I don't need to be injured to be—what was it Ms. Ulrich said at the PTA lunch—'an unusually considerate young lady.'"

"You'd need a head injury to mistake Jessica Wakefield for a 'considerate young lady,'" Steven retorted.

"Jessica," Mrs. Wakefield said, returning to the kitchen, "are you going to take something out of there, or are you just cooling off the kitchen?"

Elizabeth giggled. She loved it when her mother teased Jessica.

Elizabeth couldn't help thinking that everything had turned out extremely well. Pamela Jacobson was like a new person since the Mini Olympics. Her story had been included in *The Sweet Valley Sixers,* and everyone agreed it was great—very moving and well written. Pamela was even talking about joining the newspaper staff.

She had definitely decided to stay at Sweet Valley Middle School, and after her heroic victory the week before, she had her father's complete support. It was apparent how much the day had meant to Pamela. She was really beginning to come out of her shell, and had even made suggestions in gym class for games that she could participate in. Now that Pamela was learning to speak up for herself and her needs, Elizabeth knew she would be fine.

"What are you guys doing today?" Jessica asked, bringing a box of cereal over to the table and pouring herself a generous bowl.

Steven closed his eyes, pretending to concentrate. "Wait!" he said. "I'm seeing something . . . it's faint now, but it's getting clearer and clearer . . . it's . . . it's—"

"I can't stand it," Jessica said, rolling her eyes. "Steven, do you have any idea how stupid you look right now?"

"I'm seeing what your day looks like," Steven told her. "Something tells me it's going to be unbelievably dull."

Jessica gave him a lofty look. The truth was, she was going to spend the day with Ellen Riteman. They were going to watch the new music video her older brother had just bought, and then meet Janet and Lila at the mall. Jessica and Lila were still a little cool to each other, but Jessica had been thinking it was almost time for a truce. After all, she could stand to be generous. *She* was the one who had come out of the Mini Olympics with all the glory!

"Your ESP isn't working any more," she told Steven, pouring milk over her cereal. "You couldn't be further from the truth!"

Elizabeth had to agree. That was one thing about her twin sister. Wherever she was going and whatever she had planned, one thing was certain—Jessica's day sure wasn't going to be dull!

"I don't think I like the girls Toy Car has been using in their videos," Ellen complained. She and

Jessica were in the living room of the Ritemans' spacious stucco home.

Jessica loved the Ritemans' house. It was older than most of the homes in Sweet Valley, and it had high ceilings, large fireplaces, interesting little nooks and crannies. And the Ritemans had a great living room with wooden floors, perfect for practicing dance steps.

"What are you going to buy at the mall this afternoon?" Ellen asked. "I wouldn't mind a pair of earrings like the lead singer in Toy Car has. They're really cool."

"Your mother would die," Jessica said with a smile. She was about to add something when they heard footsteps approaching from the foyer.

"Hey, Ellen," Ellen's little brother Mark said, his face streaked with tears. "I need your help."

"What is it?" Ellen said, not sounding overjoyed. Mark was nine years old, and it seemed like he had a new crisis every minute.

"It's Leon. Whiskers ate him," Mark said sorrowfully.

"Who," Jessica said in a low voice, "is Leon?"

"Leon is Mark's pet parakeet," Ellen said.

"*Was,*" Mark said. "I hate that dumb cat! I just left Leon for one second while I was looking for his birdseed, and Whiskers jumped right in the box and—"

"Try not to think about it," Ellen said, getting to her feet and patting him comfortingly on the shoulder. "What are you doing with that?" she added, peering into the cardboard box.

"I want to bury him," Mark told her. "Will you help me?"

Ellen rolled her eyes at Jessica. "Come on, Mark. You don't want to bury him. Let's just take the box outside and—"

Mark started to cry in earnest. "I want to bury him!" he cried.

"Oh, all right," Ellen said crossly. "Come on, Jessica. It looks like we're going to have to perform a funeral before we can go to the mall." She turned off the VCR, and she and Jessica trailed Mark out to the backyard.

For the next ten minutes they followed Mark around while he selected the perfect resting place for Leon's remains. Ellen, who had her father's gardening shovel in her hands, started to look annoyed. "This is really morbid, Mark," she said at last. "If we're going to do it, let's just do it. Jessica and I have to go someplace."

"OK," Mark said at last, stopping under a tree at the end of the yard. "Right here!"

Ellen came over and handed him the shovel. "You dig," she instructed.

"OK," Mark said. "But first I have to read the service."

"Oh, boy," Ellen said, throwing herself down on the grass. Jessica sat down too.

Mark read out loud from something he had

written on a piece of paper in his pocket. He described Leon in great detail—where Mark had bought him, how much he cost, what kind of food he liked. "It's too bad Leon died before he learned how to speak," Mark added, looking mournful.

Jessica and Ellen clapped respectfully. "Now why don't you start digging," Ellen instructed.

Mark started to dig. "I think I hit a root or something," he said a minute later. "The shovel is sticking."

"Just keep digging—it'll be OK," Ellen said, not really paying attention.

"Maybe it's a rock," Mark said. "The shovel is sticking against something. Listen—it's making a funny noise."

Jessica looked interested. She had heard Elizabeth describe something like this from one of the Amanda Howard mysteries she was always reading. "Let me try," she said, taking the shovel from Mark.

Sure enough, the shovel struck something hard. It sounded like metal. Jessica dug deeper, and after several minutes of exertion, she had cleared away enough dirt to see the edge of something made of gray metal.

"It's a box!" Mark cried, peering down into the hole.

Ellen and Jessica exchanged glances. "Back up, Mark," Ellen said. "Let me see it."

Soon she and Jessica had lifted the small

metal box from the hole and brushed the dirt off it. It wasn't very large, but it was heavy, and securely locked.

"Wow!" Mark said. "It's buried treasure!"

Jessica gave Ellen a significant look. "Mark," Ellen said, "I think we should bury Leon now. We'll worry about this later." She put the box down beside her.

Mark eyed it uneasily. "We can wait to bury Leon," he told her. "I want to open the box."

"Later," Ellen said, "Come on, Mark. We can't interrupt a *funeral*."

Jessica knew she and Ellen were thinking the same thing. They wanted to find out what was inside that box. And they wanted to make sure whatever it was, they kept it away from Mark.

Especially if it really *did* turn out to be buried treasure!

***What is inside the box? Find out in Sweet Valley Twins #11,* BURIED TREASURE.**